AF439213

A GROOM FOR GRACIE

BLIZZARD BRIDES SERIES #11

HEATHER BLANTON

A Groom for Gracie The Blizzard Brides Book 11

DISCLAIMER

All the characters described in this story are fictional. They are not based on any real persons, past or present. Any resemblance to real persons, living or deceased, is coincidental and unintended.

All rights reserved.

No part of this book may be reproduced in any form or by any electronic or mechanical means, including information storage and retrieval systems, without written permission from the author, except for the use of brief quotations in a book review.

Copyright © 2021 HEATHER BLANTON

All rights reserved.

A big thank you to Lisa Coffield, Amy Petrowich, and Trudy Cordle for reading and editing this book, and Erin Dameron Hill for designing the beautiful cover!

A GROOM FOR GRACIE

She's a Card Sharp, a Pickpocket, and an Actress…
Well, Nobody's Perfect.

If Gracie Erstwhile wants to keep her new homestead, she must do what every other widow in Last Chance, NE has done: choose a mail-order groom. At least having a man around to handle the farm will free her up to pursue her dream of opening a theater.

Noble McCain has lost his wife and his farm. And while he doesn't "need" a wife, his son needs a mother. He agrees to run Gracie's farm and believes he and the little actress have come to an acceptable arrangement—acceptable until Noble realizes Gracie has some pretty shady ways.

When she agrees to put on a theatrical presentation for Last Chance, she gets a glimpse at a new life. She makes friends, guides a son, and chases a dream—why, she might even be falling in love.

It's all going along so well…until Gracie's past catches up with her.

PROLOGUE

August, 1878

GRACIE ERSTWHILE PRESSED the phony mustache over her lip and then pulled back from the mirror for a better look. The wagon's dim lamp cast long, sickly-looking shadows under her eyes and she scrunched her nose up in distaste. "I look awful." But the glue was holding.

"Good. All the more reason my elixir will heal you."

Gracie studied her husband, Melvin, in the mirror, tying his tie, getting ready in their cramped, little wagon. Getting ready for another show. One last chance to bamboozle some innocent folks out of their hard-earned dollars. And she would help him.

She didn't hate her life. Yet, some days it felt…tawdry. Shallow. Maybe even wrong.

She sighed quietly as she turned away from the mirror and twisted all her long, golden hair up into a tight bun. Next, she reached for her hat sitting on the bed and tucked it on tight. She brushed her hands down her jacket, pulled her trousers a little higher and nodded. "I'm ready. I look all right?"

Melvin paused slipping into his coat—a garish, cream-colored affair with bright red piping and pants to match. Lord, how had she ever thought it was a nice suit? He twisted his long mustache as he assessed her with a critical eye. "Yes, you look fine. Now be sure to stay in the back. The very back. And you know your cue?"

"Yes." Of course she did. Why did he always feel the need to ask her that? Gracie tugged on the hat again. It was tight, secure, but something wasn't quite right. A little frustrated, she snugged the Stetson lower. Testing it, she wiggled her head in an exaggerated way, but the hat remained in place. *It will do*, she told herself. "I'll see you in an hour."

GRACIE HATED WHAT CAME NEXT. She had to hide in the shadows until enough of a crowd formed in front of their wagon that she could slip up unnoticed. She glanced uneasily up and down the side of the building she was leaning on. Barrels and crates were stacked precariously on both sides of her. Last week in Topeka, she'd hidden in a spot similar to this, but sat on the ground cross-legged. A rat had boldly skittered across her lap and she'd nearly screamed like a pigtailed little girl. A response that would have announced to the whole town she was a fake and so was Dr. Melvin Erstwhile and his Fantabulous Miraculous Amazing All-Healing Magical Elixir.

She did not care to repeat the experience, so she would stand. Besides, the moment she was waiting for made up for all the dark, dank hiding places.

Something pressed on her leg and she nearly squealed, but realized a stray cat had joined her. She squatted down and petted the skinny, little tabby. "I'm sorry, I wish I had a nice fat mouse for you." Gracie also wished she had a cat. Or a dog. She wished she stayed in one place long enough to have a pet of any kind.

She stood back up with a sigh. Melvin said soon. Soon they would have a farm and be stable, solid citizens somewhere. Gracie thought she might get a kitten then.

The stagnant summer air here in Abilene was stifling, and she wiped sweat off her lip, hating the heavy clothes she had to wear. Across the street, Melvin had placed a placard in front of their wagon announcing the next show at 7:00 pm. A small, make-shift stage set on tackle blocks waited for him. It would elevate him only a few inches over the audience, but it always seemed to be enough.

Finally, a crowd was forming. A romantic-looking couple strolling arm-in-arm stopped out of curiosity. A fat, banker-looking fella in a nice suit, twirling his pocket watch, paused, checked the time, and seemed to decide he could spare a few minutes. A couple of lanky, laughing cowboys wandered up, talking loudly, reading the slogans on the side of the wagon.

"Cures all lumbagos and boils…Eases…" The cowboy tilted his head and rested his hand on his gun "Eases in… intest…inal distress—"

"Shorty coulda used that the other night." The second cowboy heehawed and then picked up the reading. "All forms of liver complaints and constipation. No sore it will not heal. No pain it will not subdue."

The man with the gun grimaced. "Bet it tastes like horse pi—"

"I've been told the worse it tastes the better it works. I got an aunt in Kansas City who swears by her tonics."

The first cowboy thoughtfully crossed his arms over his chest. "Could use some maybe to keep in the chuck wagon then. If it's any account."

Gracie nonchalantly ambled over and stood beside them. "I heard Dr. Erstwhile's elixir is the best in three states." She did not look at the men directly, but she could see them out of the corner of her eye. The cowboy with the gun had a deep scar down his cheek. "Least that's what my grandma said." She shoved her hands into her pockets and rocked on her heels, keeping her energy level low to feign her upcoming sickness.

One of the cowboys sized her up. "Your grandma, huh?"

"Yep. Sent me down here to buy her a couple of bottles. She swears by it. Says it soothes her arthritis and she sleeps real sound after a glass." Gracie casually touched her mustache, double-checking to make sure the glue had dried. "She said it would help me, too."

"What's the matter with you?"

"Don't know. Sick to my stomach."

The cowboy with the long scar took off his hat and shook dark, sweat-matted hair off his forehead. "Our cook suffers bad with arthritis. Makes him crabby." He replaced the hat. "He won't bake pies when it flares up."

Gracie didn't push. She knew the marks had to come to their own conclusions—what they *thought* were their own conclusions.

"How old's your grandma, boy?"

"Seventy," Gracie said, pleased they were so sure of her gender.

"Seventy? She's doing good."

"Yep. She credits this elixir with her health and good spirits. I'm looking forward to finding out for myself."

The cowboy grunted in a thoughtful way and Gracie licked her lips to keep from smiling. The two cowboys put their heads together and muttered about money and bottles and how much was pie worth. A moment later, one of them looked at her again. "You know how much the bottles cost?"

"Um, well, my grandma gave me five dollars and told me I could get three bottles for that."

"Five dollars," one of the cowboys yelped.

"Yeah, but," Gracie added quickly, "I hear the doctor makes deals. Offers specials."

The cowboys settled down a little. Gracie didn't think the stingy cowboys were a good sign but she was at least happy to be acting. She loved pretending. One day she'd be up on a real stage again performing Shakespeare or Ibsen. One day.

She let her mind stroll back to theaters and plays and stage lights as the crowd filled in around her. She noted the increasing size of the audience here and knew Melvin would be pleased.

He would keep them in suspense for another few minutes, however. He never took the stage on time.

Occupying herself, she was reliving her performance in *Romeo and Juliet* at a theater in Philadelphia, when Melvin leaped from the back of the wagon and bounded up on the stage. He moved like a deer but Gracie knew the movement cost him. His back had been spasming lately and nothing they'd tried had helped. Not even the elixir. So much for miracles.

"Ladies and gentlemen," he said, using his fine, baritone voice and fluid, almost hypnotic hand gestures, "tonight your lives will change. They will never be the same." His voice rose and fell as if he were quoting King Lear. "I have with me the most fantastic, most fabulous medical cure known to man…"

Gracie let his voice fade. She drifted back to a fine theater in San Francisco, where she'd seen that wonderful production of My Distant Love. The dramatic lighting had awed her, the acting wooed her nearly into a swoon. That was the play that had given her the fever. Oh, how she wanted to act…

"I say," Melvin repeated, an edge only Gracie would recognize in his voice, "Is there anyone here who suffers from neuralgia or stomach issues?"

Gracie's hand shot up. "I do, mister. I got dyspepsia."

"Well, come on up, son! Let me give you a free sample. It'll clear you right up."

Gracie made her way through the small, but tight, crowd, bumping into a few people here and there, mumbling apologies. Her hands were fast and subtle. The strangers never felt their pocket watches or money clips leave their person. A moment later, she stepped up on the small stage, pressing a hand to her stomach. "I've been on the verge of vomiting for three days, sir. You sure your magical elixir can heal me?"

"I've no doubt, my boy." Melvin nodded at the crowd with great confidence. "Just watch this, folks." Melvin pulled a bottle from a group of three boxes stacked on top of each other. "Dr. Erstwhile's Fantabulous Miraculous Amazing All-Healing Magical Elixir will turn this boy into a new man."

"I sure hope so," Gracie moaned. "I've been puny for days."

Melvin produced a shot glass from his coat and poured Gracie two fingers. If she hadn't been nauseated before, this would do it. The elixir was awful. It tasted like she imagined sweaty socks might.

But this is acting, she thought and took the glass. *Hiding what you really think. Becoming a whole new person.* She twitched an eyebrow at Melvin, tossed back the drink and closed her eyes. Consciously, she traced the burn of the insidious liquid down her throat, past her lungs, into her stomach. She ignored the taste, instead thinking of apple pies and sugar cookies. Anything but what had just raced down her gullet.

Still envisioning sugar cookies, she moaned and touched her stomach. The crowd was riveted into place, silent, and still as corpses. Oh, but she could feel their wide, curious gazes. She could also feel the choking bile rising up in her throat. The elixir was a torture to drink.

A consummate actress, she moaned again, but added a subtle upbeat note to it at the end. Then she moaned once more, a sound of peace, wholeness, relief, and opened her eyes.

"Doctor Erstwhile, I feel..." The crowd leaned in. "I feel..." Closer. "I feel like I could..." Suddenly Gracie did a no-hands cartwheel off the stage and landed on one knee in the dirt, arms outstretched, the audience barely having time to clear the space. "I feel like a new person!"

The crowd gasped. Then the clapping and hollering broke out. The marks rushed the stage, bumping into Gracie, jostling her about. She pressed her now loosened hat back in place and pulled a five-dollar bill from her pocket. "Three bottles, Dr. Erstwhile!" She waved the money. "I must have three bottles!"

Gracie elbowed her way in front of the fat banker and took her purchases from Melvin, who messaged approval of her with an infinitesimal nod. She did not respond with any telltale sign. Instead, she thanked him for the elixirs and hurried away from the pressing crowd clamoring excitedly for their own magical tonic. Hands waved cash in the air. Men jostled each other. The distracted audience was easy pickings, but she admonished herself not to be greedy.

Holding the elixirs in one arm, she slipped her hand into her pocket and touched the watch, the gold money clip, and a coin she'd pilfered. The night had turned out to be more successful than she'd expected. Of course, they still had to get out of Abilene.

She returned to her hiding place. Pressed deeper in the shadows, she watched Melvin trying to get rid of the last customers. The mustache tickled her nose, so she peeled it off carefully and stowed it in her chest pocket…and waited some more.

In another ten or so minutes, Melvin was alone and packing up. He put the remaining elixir in the back of their wagon and stowed the small stage on specially built hooks beneath the bed. He tucked the tackle blocks in a storage box and then turned and peered down the dark, empty street. He looked this way and that…Nothing moved. This end of Abilene was dead. He nodded in Gracie's direction.

Ready to get out of town and hit the hay somewhere down the road, she was hotfooting it across the intersection toward her husband when a man yelled. "You there!"

She pretended not to hear, but Melvin's wide eyes communicated the danger. She picked up speed as he spun and headed to the front of the wagon.

"I said you there, boy. Stop."

A hand latched onto Gracie's shoulder, spun her violently. The cowboy with the scar glared at her. "My money," he demanded, gouging strong, slender fingers into her shoulders. "Now, or I'll call the sheriff."

"I don't know what you're talking about, mister.

He shook her violently, rattling her teeth. One of the bottles slipped from her grasp and shattered on the ground. "My money!"

Her hand flew up instinctively to keep her hat on but the man knocked it away and the hat and her hair tumbled free.

For a moment he looked purely thunderstruck, then his expression darkened. "You little con—"

He stopped in mid-sentence, his eyes rolled backwards, and he collapsed to the ground like a rag doll. Gracie jumped back, shocked. And then she saw Melvin standing there with a sock full of marbles—his favorite weapon—poised to strike again. But the cowboy didn't move.

"Come on." Melvin grabbed her arm. "We have to get out of here."

"Is he dead?"

"Nah, just out cold. We gotta move."

1

———

Gracie patted the envelopes into a nice, neat stack and placed them in the center of the small coffee table. Pastor Collin's brow knit together with clear disapproval. He was a dandy with a weak chin and an overrated sense of importance. In Gracie's humble opinion. Yet, she was aware he carried weight in Last Chance.

The pastor leaned forward. "Mrs. Erstwhile—" A few of the guests in the hotel glanced over at him. Chagrinned, he cleared his throat and lowered his voice. "Pardon me. I'm somewhat passionate about this topic, as you know. The Good Lord has intended for women to marry. Last Chance is no place for a pretty, young widow on her own."

Gracie shifted on the settee, but didn't take her stubborn gaze from the pushy pastor. "I understand. I am still trying to decide my future."

He sighed heavily and leaned back in the plush, velvet chair. "Perhaps I can help you along. I was having an amicable chat with Mr. Bently from the surveyor's office. He mentioned that the window for you to claim your homestead was closing in ten days. I was surprised to learn your husband had not completed the paperwork."

Gracie swallowed. In the death and tragedy wreaked by the blizzard, she'd forgotten all about the details of land claims. "The day we arrived, he learned of the hunt and jumped in to help. We had time to take our wagon out to the land, get a room in town, and then he left."

And just like that, Gracie was a widow. A widow with a hundred and sixty acres, a wagon, and a small supply of money this hotel was depleting. Quickly. The pastor was right. She had to stop vacillating.

Only now, she didn't even have the land, apparently.

"You understand, you must be married to claim it." Pastor Collins twirled his hat in his hands in a fidgety way that annoyed Grace. "A widow would have been eligible to take over the land as head of household. Only, your husband never completed the filing."

"We thought we had time." The words sounded bleak and somber now, devoid of hope.

He reached out and picked up the letters on the table. "In the Lord's mercy, I believe *you* do. Someone in this stack may be close at hand and can be here in a matter of a few days. Or…there is always the possibility of a local?" Pastor Collins raised his eyebrows, clearly communicating his intent. "Should the Lord lead you thus, I'm more than ready to make my contribution to the future of Last Chance by taking a bride. And I am quite the catch."

Grace's stomach rolled. The idea of marrying the pastor or

any other stranger was bad enough, but to marry out of desperation? She couldn't do it. Slowly, she rose to her feet and the pastor with her. "I can't marry under these conditions. I'd like very much to keep the land. It would be a wise investment, but the price is too high."

His face fell. "Are you sure? You haven't even opened the letters." He handed them to her. "Why don't you spend some time in prayer, and then at least read through them before you make a firm decision. I hope you don't mind. I took the liberty of adding one from myself. It's on top."

Gracie smiled, took the letters, and stumbled as she came around the coffee table. Pastor Collins caught her and she effortlessly relieved him of his pocket watch. "Oh, pardon me," she said, stepping back and dropping the item in her pocket.

"Quite all right," he said smiling dreamily.

GRACIE WANDERED the streets of Last Chance, fingers clutching the letters, her mind a whirl. Before she realized it, she was at the stage depot. The late fall day was nice, only hinting at a breeze. The sun shone down on the wide open, vast and tree-less landscape on the other side of the North Platte River. Hard to believe little more than a month ago the snow had buried the first floor of the hotel, the river had frozen solid, and the temperature had dropped so low so fast animals had turned to blocks of ice standing on their feet.

And somewhere out there, twenty-some men had been taken by the storm as well. She wondered if Melvin had been helpful or had spent the whole trip trying to sell something. Not a bad man, he had been single-minded about…*the deal.* The finesse of the deal, he'd called it. The ability to sway and manipulate people had obsessed him. The first years of their marriage, Gracie had seen him as a sort of God, or at least a man with near-mystical powers.

Then she'd realized he was simply a man with few morals and the gift of persuasion. He'd taught her a lot of things about the huckster's life, but not much about life in general. Especially around nice folks. She stopped and sighed, looking around the little town.

"He's right," she whispered, thinking of the pastor. "This is no place for a woman alone." She smacked the letters against the palm of her hand and dropped on to the bench in front of the depot. Just holding them made her uncomfortable, and she laid them beside her, face down. Then she wondered why she'd placed them so. Was she afraid? Did reading them mean she'd surrendered to this horrible idea?

"Well, it wouldn't hurt to just read them, I guess." *Maybe,* she thought, *there's a rich Prince Charming in there who wants to farm and toil and roll around in the dirt, so his wife can build a little community theater.*

The idea was absurd but possible, of course.

"Afternoon."

A young boy, thirteen or so, scrunching his hat, startled her out of her daydreaming. "Oh, good afternoon."

"Mind if I have a seat?" He grinned, showing astonishingly white teeth against his tanned skin. Dark hair glistened in the sun's glare. Gracie suspected Spanish blood in his background.

She motioned beside her. "Please."

He settled and took a moment to scan the town. "Bigger than I thought. Still not much to speak of, though."

"No, Last Chance is not New York City, that's for certain. You moving here?"

He squinted at her. "I guess that'll be up to Pa."

"It's a nice town for a family." The moment the words left Gracie's mouth, she saw the boy's expression falter and she knew she'd misspoke.

"I think my ma would have liked it."

"Oh, um, yes." The conversation lagged awkwardly, and

she decided it needed some levity. Besides, she needed the practice. She turned to the boy. "It's a prosperous town. Why, we have money falling out of our ears!"

"What?" He tilted his head and stared at her with open skepticism. "You're pulling my leg."

"No, I can prove it." In one swift, perfect movement she touched the boy's ear and flicked the nickel between her fingers. "See." The boy's eyes went wide as a harvest moon as he took the coin. She hadn't lost her touch.

"Keep it," she said when he offered it back. "Came out of your ear, not mine."

While he was completely stunned by the illusion, he wasn't fooled by it. "That's one heck of a trick. Can you teach me?"

Gracie was impressed by the question. Every single time she'd performed it for children, they always asked her to do it again. Give them more money. Not this young man. She thought it boded well for his future. Today, however, she didn't have the time. She had decisions to make. "I'm sorry, not today." She picked up the letters and the boy's eyes went round again.

"You are her. I thought so."

"I beg your pardon?"

"We've come a long way looking for you," he said, jumping to his feet. "Pa left everything behind. At least you're a pretty bride." He glanced around Last Chance and his smile faded. "Even if the town ain't much. Well, any way, my name is Matt."

"Listen, son," Gracie stood. "You're confused. I'm nobody's bride. I'm not even sure I'm staying in this two-bit, dusty town."

The boy gestured at the letters in her hand, of which the top one had *Blizzard Brides* written boldly on it. "I know that envelope. And you were supposed to meet us here at the depot." His good humor evaporated instantly, and his expression became that of a wounded puppy. "Is it me? You don't want a son? That it?"

"No, you don't understand—"

"I'm a real hard worker. I do my chores. I'm a lot of help on a farm—"

Gracie waved her hands back and forth. "Stop. Just stop and let me get a word in." But there wasn't much to say. "I'm nobody's bride." She charged past him rudely, but something about the boy panicked her. "I'm nobody's bride," she repeated over her shoulder as she hurried down the boardwalk.

FLUSTERED, Gracie wasn't sure where she was going till she saw the sign for the surveyor's office. The words *You're her?* followed her all the way, haunted her. But the sign hanging over the door knocked them right out of her head. Maybe if she heard her situation from the horse's mouth, she could think more clearly. Surely getting married wasn't the only way.

She let herself into the dark office, and resisted an urge to raise the blinds. She gave her eyes a moment to adjust and spotted the U.S. land agent. He looked up from his paperwork. "Yes, ma'am." He rose and walked over, his hand out. "How can I help you?

After shaking his hand, Gracie peered a little closer at the man. "You don't remember me? The Erstwhiles. I'm Gracie Erstwhile."

"Oh, yes, ma'am. Now I do. Shouldn't have forgotten. I don't have too many pretty faces in here, you know."

"Yes, well, I was talking to Pastor Collins earlier today. He said I was running out of time to file my homestead claim."

"Oh, you're the one. Yes, ma'am. I happened to mention to him you were going to lose your standing, if you didn't do something. It's the last one on the books and I have to finish it off."

"What do you mean it's the last one?"

"For a head of household."

"I'm sorry, I'm still confused. What are you saying?"

"It's the last one-hundred-and-sixty-acre tract the government has here, but it has to be claimed by the head of the household. Your husband didn't finish the paperwork and I understand…" He proceeded gently here. "Well, I understand he perished with the others. So, either you've got to get married and finish this paperwork or the claim goes back to the public."

Gracie took a step back as if the information had made the temperature in the room soar. She had to get married to stay here. She had to get married to claim the land. Or she had to leave. And go back to where? To what?

Gracie's heart was racing, and she felt both flushed and faint at the same moment. Why did it feel as if life was conspiring against her? She'd been moving around since she was sixteen. Melvin had promised to settle her here. Give her a home.

"Ma'am?"

"I'm sorry." She needed fresh air. "I need a few moments to ponder things. I'll be back."

"You've only got a few days—"

"I know," she said opening the door and slipping outside. "I know."

The letters were wrinkling in her sweaty hands. She looked at them as if they held a death sentence. But she didn't know that for certain. Maybe there was a Prince Charm—

"Mrs. Thompson, I'll have a word with you."

A man's voice, ill-tempered and loud, drew her attention down the walk to the boy, Matt, and a strikingly tall, muscular man walking toward her. He wore a good scowl on an otherwise handsome, chiseled face. Angry, dark eyes drilled into her and she tensed, ready to run.

"I made it clear on numerous occasions I had a son and would be bringing him with me. For you to back out on our agreement is allowable, certainly, but not for this reason. I'm offended by your dishonesty."

She patted the air between them. "There is clearly a misunderstanding here. I'm not the woman you're looking for."

He cut his eyes at the letters in her hand, the words *Blizzard Brides* obvious. "You're one of the brides and you were at the depot at noon. But you want me to believe you're not Mrs. Willa Thompson?"

"Practically every woman in town is a mail-order bride. And I was at the depot by...happenstance. Furthermore, I happen to know that Willa Thompson left town last week. As the bride of a dry goods salesman."

She hadn't meant to blurt that out, but there it was, and it impacted the man. His jaw went slack, his shoulders fell a little, then he looked down at his son. "You didn't ask this lady's name?"

"No, I just thought—

"You just thought."

"Well, she was at the depot, like you said. And she has a stack of those letters." The boy glanced at Gracie, as if for help.

"My name is Gracie Erstwhile..." She waved off the controversy and patted Matt on the shoulder. "It was an easy mistake to make."

"Well, I..." The man whipped off his stained gray cowboy hat, ruffling wavy, caramel colored hair. He stepped in closer and lowered his head in a contrite manner. A big man, his mass astonished Gracie. His broad chest and red flannel shirt swallowed her field of vision. "I owe you an apology. Sorry for the misunderstanding. It's just that it took the last of everything we had to get here and…now…she's not even here." He squeezed his son's shoulder. "But we'll be fine. We'll sleep in the livery tonight and figure things out in the morning. How's that sound?"

"Like an adventure. Haven't slept in the barn in a long time."

"All right then. Sorry for the trouble, ma'am." The tall stranger tipped his hat at Gracie and he and the boy turned to head down the walk.

Even as she shook her head to wave away their predicament—and hers—an idea danced in her brain. With every step the man took, an inexplicable urgency cried out in her to stop him, but she fought the nudge until it became a shove. "Excuse me!"

The man and the boy pivoted back to face her.

"Are you by any chance a farmer?"

They took two uncertain steps in her direction. "All my life," the father said, "but with two hailstorms, a fire, and my wife's sickness, I wound up losing my place in Kansas. Mrs. Thompson and I had planned to use the Homestead Act and the Timber Culture Act to get some land near Kearney."

Gracie chewed on her lip. Tapped her toe. Like a hot air balloon, the idea grew larger and larger in her head. The man quirked an eyebrow, curious. This was absurd, she told herself. Crazy. Foolhardy.

But most of her crazy and fool-hardy decisions had worked out.

She crossed the distance between them and addressed man and boy equally. "I have a business proposition for you."

The man leaned back and crossed his arms. "We're listening."

"I have the paperwork started on a claim to one-hundred and sixty acres here. My husband died before we completed it." She hurried past their sympathetic looks. "For me to retain the claim, I have to have a husband." She inched closer and lowered her voice. "What I really need is someone who could work the farm. Make it profitable. My true heart's desire is to someday open a theatre."

Mr. McCain's eyes had glimmered with interest until that moment. The light turned to suspicion. "A theater? You mean you'd want to sell the farm?"

"Um, I don't know exactly. Possibly. Or possibly if the farm did well, I could rent or buy a building with our profits. I hadn't thought that far ahead. I just know I shouldn't let go of the land if I don't have to."

"Ma'am, it takes a while to get a farm producing. It could be years before you'd even have any spare cash."

"She could make extra money doing her magic tricks, Pa," Matt interjected with glee. "Show him. Show Pa where the money comes from around here." The boy wiggled his brow. "Go ahead, Mrs.—gee, what is your name?"

"Gracie Erstwhile." She smiled. She couldn't help it. She adored the boy's enthusiasm. She slid her gaze up, up, up, across the field of flannel to look Mr. McCain in the eye. He was so tall…and handsome. "I'm not sure I can reach his ears."

"Yes, you can. Try."

Gracie chuckled. "You see, Mr. McCain, Last Chance is a prosperous town. We literally have money…" She reached up and as her fingers lightly brushed his cheek, the world stopped for an instant. His eyes, brown as her morning coffee, seemed to hold sweet and intoxicating secrets. Gracie blinked and finished the trick, palming the nickel and flashing it to them. "…falling out of our ears."

The man grinned and took the nickel from her. "I won't lie, that's pretty impressive." He gave her back the money. "But parlor tricks won't get a ranch or a theater off the ground. And having a body around that's not pulling her weight would only make it that much harder."

"Oh, I intend to work the farm as well. At first. I understand I can't make dreams happen overnight." He studied her. She studied him right back.

"She'll lose the land if she doesn't do something, Pa."

"You all right with this idea? Just being farm hands?"

"No, don't look at it like that," Gracie corrected firmly. "Partners. I supply the land. You supply most of the labor. Then, when we start on the theater, well, it will be from our profits. Not until we can afford it, and we'll negotiate the amount."

2

Noble shoved his hands into his pockets and ambled over to the edge of the boardwalk. He'd come here to get married. Well, that wasn't exactly true. Marriage was not his sole reason. It was a vehicle to getting his life back on the right track. And after agreeing to things, the little gal had gone back on her word and run off with a salesman.

Guess it wasn't meant to be, huh, Lord. But what about this one?

He turned and studied the young lady. She was lithe, graceful, like a cat, and moved with immense confidence. He'd noticed that even before he'd taken in her jade eyes, petite features, and shimmering blonde hair. She wore it in a long, messy braid that didn't seem to fit with her mannerisms. Maybe she was having the kind of day he'd been having for the last two years.

He was relieved Mrs. Thompson had skedaddled. She wasn't Jessie. No one would be. Ever. But Matt needed a mother. The concern that drove Noble. What was best for his son? Was this it? "So, this wouldn't be a marriage?"

"No, and I hope I'm making that clear."

"Suits me. Better than the arrangement I would have had with Mrs. Thompson." Since he was never going to fall in love again, he didn't want or need anything else from a marriage. He ran his gaze over Mrs. Erstwhile, looking for signs of what kind of person she was. He did insist on honesty. "She turned out to be a liar. I don't know you, Mrs. Erstwhile. I don't know your character. I was only considering the arrangement for Matt's sake. Having a woman around. You understand."

Mrs. Erstwhile took several seconds to reply, giving careful consideration to her next statement, he assumed. "I can tell you whatever we agree to, I will be a solid, loyal partner. One you can trust."

Now, that *was* what he wanted and needed. Yet, he couldn't shake the feeling she was playing some kind of word game with him. "Solid, loyal, trustworthy." The words were all good. Had sound meaning and promise. Still…

"Can I say the same about you?" she asked.

"Solid. Loyal. Trustworthy," he repeated, examining each word. He was all these things and nodded. He was also lonely, but there would be no getting around that. Jessie was gone and he couldn't imagine having those feelings for any other woman.

Matt's head was on a swivel and Noble bit down on a smile. The boy somehow had quickly decided this matter and was in the lady's corner. Slowly, Noble offered the woman his hand. "Let's take care of the paperwork."

Gracie stared for a moment as if she'd never made a deal before. As she started to accept his grasp, a horrifying thought crossed Noble's mind and he pulled back. "Are you a God-fearing woman, Mrs. Erstwhile? That's important."

"My husband was not a Godly man. I did not attend church whilst married to him. I would be happy if that situation changed."

Again he had the sense she was being very particular with her words. Beside him, Matt's smile grew so big Noble mused it might overtake the boy's face, especially when he watched the two adults shake hands.

"My Christian name is Noble, Mrs. Erstwhile. Noble McCain."

She ducked her head in acknowledgement and said, "Please, call me Gracie."

3

———

"So which way is the preacher?"

"Preacher?" Gracie barely kept the panic out of her voice. "Would you mind if we didn't—I mean if we used a justice-of-the-peace instead? It strikes me as more…appropriate."

Noble rubbed his neck, glanced at his son. "Well, I guess. Sure. This is, after all, more of a partnership than a m—"

"Exactly." Gracie didn't even want to hear the word. Married. Marriage. Marrying. What she and Noble were doing was just a business deal. Like her association with Melvin had become in the last four years of their time together. All business. Even their intimacy had drifted into a perfunctory function. "But I didn't expect this, as you can imagine." And while she was panicked by what she was doing…there was also an underlying sense that this truly was her next step. "Could you meet me at the courthouse in about an hour? I'd like to…" *Pull myself together.* "Freshen up a bit."

Noble squinted at her, suspicion oozing from him. "You sure about this? If you're going to back out, I'd rather you do it now."

"No, I'm not—" Matt's gaze, full of hope and admiration eased her churning emotions a little. He was encouraging and Gracie liked him immensely. "I'll be there."

"Reckon we can neaten up some, too." Noble dragged his fingers over a stubbly jaw. "Let's make ourselves look a little more presentable, Matt. This town has a barber?"

"Yes, down on Main Street."

"All right then." He dropped a hand on Matt's shoulder. "In an hour."

GRACIE HURRIED to her room in the hotel, slammed the door behind her, and leaned back on the wood, sweaty hands squeezing the doorknob. Her heart beat wildly in her chest, but it wasn't from the run down the street. What had she gotten herself into?

A marriage that wasn't real. Under a name that wasn't really hers. Following on the heels of a life of lies. Layer upon layer of deceit. When would it end?

But what were her choices? She was Gracie Erstwhile now. She had no place to go. She and Melvin had picked Last Chance because it was out of the way, the land was clear for staking a claim, their money would see them through for a bit. And eventually they'd build her theater and make money from it. Best of all, the ghost of Professor Erstwhile and his reputation would quietly fade away with the passage of time. People would forget.

Gracie tried to argue one last time she could take the money and run. Buy a dress shop in some little town. Of course, that would use all of the money. Not to mention, she didn't know how to run a dress shop. No, the land here was the anchor. And now she had a man who could farm it. A manager. She just had to marry him. That was all. An arrangement on paper.

And Noble McCain was a safe bet. She'd learned to read people in her years of acting and then playing the plant in the medicine show. She suspected his biggest vice might be reading his Bible too late into the evening. Boring but harmless.

"WELL, this is fine, Mrs. Erstwhile. I'm glad to see you've found a respondent for the ad." Judge Bringegar rose from his desk and walked around to shake her hand. He looked up at Noble and then down at Matt. "Looks like he comes with a ready-made family, too. I bet you're a lot of help, aren't you, son?"

"I think so." Matt cut his eyes up at his father, as if daring him to argue.

"But why aren't you using Pastor Collins?" The judge asked.

"Um, well," Gracie stammered and Noble averted his eyes. "This isn't—"

"Forgive my manners." The judge threw up his hand. "Isn't any of my business." He strode back around to his side of the desk, sat, and began rifling through the drawers. "You get married anywhere you want. I'm just as legal as the pastor, if not as cloaked in religion."

Noble scowled at the remark. Gracie understood he didn't seem to like this very much but was going along. "What all do you need for our ma—union to be legal, Judge?" she asked.

"Oh, just a little paperwork, a witness, and an oath." He held up a sheet of paper, scanned it, nodded. "Here we are. Now first," he reached for the fountain pen on his desk and plucked it from its holder. "Mrs. Erstwhile, I need your name."

"My name?"

"Yes, your name." He poised the pen, ready to write it down.

"My married name?"

Judge Bringegar looked up through fuzzy eyebrows. He was a little puzzled or annoyed, Gracie wasn't sure which. "What name you go by, yes."

"I go by Gracie Erstwhile."

"No middle name or maiden name?"

"Gracie Erstwhile." She could feel the heat in Noble's stare, but she didn't look at him. She hadn't lied. Exactly. Yet, she suspected he suspected something in her awkward replies.

"And what about you, sir?"

"Noble Gabriel McCain."

The judge hummed softly as he wrote. "And you, boy, you the witness?"

"Can I, Pa?"

"Sure."

"I'm Matthew Martin McCain."

"All right." The judge finished, picked up his Bible and rejoined the couple. "Simple ceremony or lengthy and fancy?"

"Simple is fine with me." Gracie checked with Noble and he nodded.

Something seemed to dawn on the judge. A knowing glimmer came into his eyes. "I understand. If you'd hold hands, please."

Gracie tried to ignore the comfortable way her hand

slipped into Noble's. And she marveled for an instant how small hers looked in his.

The judge cleared his throat. "Do you, Noble Gabriel McCain, take this woman to be your lawfully wedded wife?"

"I do."

"And do you, Gracie Erstwhile, take this man to be your lawfully wedded husband?"

"I do."

"Then by the power vested in me by the great state of Nebraska, I pronounce you both husband and wife. You may kiss your bride."

The statement froze Gracie and Noble. Their eyes locked and she saw her fear reflected back at her. Noble licked his lips and quickly leaned down and touched his lips to hers. Literally, a spark of static electricity arced between them and both backed up with a start.

Judge Bringegar laughed richly and slapped Noble in the ribs. "That's a good omen, son. A very good omen."

Matt wandered down the street looking over this new town. Taking a bite of the licorice stick in his hand, he wondered how things would go between Pa and Miss Gracie. He missed his ma still, but he was forgetting what she looked liked. For nights on end, he'd walked out into the cornfield to be alone, to cry, and to grieve her passing. And then one night he'd slept till dawn.

It made him feel guilty. Especially when he knew his pa was up at all hours of the night even now.

Matt was glad Mrs. Thompson had left town. That had never felt right in his opinion, but he felt differently about Miss Gracie.

She was too pretty not to like. And that magic trick of hers…

Matt smiled to himself. He couldn't wait to learn how she did that. He stopped and peered at a new saddle sitting in the window at the saddlery. Pretty thing. Lots of latigo on it. Maybe when Pa and Miss Gracie were done getting supplies, he'd get them down here to see it. Wouldn't be a bad Christmas present. Matt could use a new saddle.

"I've never seen you before."

Matt turned. A boy close in age, with a dirty face and pretty worn clothes, was leaning on the end of the building and staring with a challenging tilt to his chin.

"That's 'cause I'm new in town. Just got here today."

Nose up, shoulders straight, the boy walked over, moving like he was some kind prince or something, like a royal robe trailed behind him. He surveyed Matt top to bottom and back again. "You gonna be a problem?"

"I don't know. I don't think so."

"My name is Bartholomew G. Branson. Me and my boys, we have a little gang. We get what we want when we want it. Savvy?"

Matt did *not* savvy and shook his head.

"We want candy, we take it. We want a steak from the butcher we take it. All the kids in town either stay out of our way or run with us. So, I ask again, you gonna be a problem?"

Matt had never met any kid like Bartholomew. He was bold, confident, and kinda swaggered around like an outlaw. Matt wasn't awestruck, but close. "I don't reckon I'll be a problem."

"You wanna run with us?"

"I don't know. Maybe."

"I don't ask everybody. But you look like you can handle yourself."

"I can."

"If you wanna join up, you have to prove your loyalty."

"Prove it? How?"

"Go into the mercantile and swipe a piece of candy."

"Swipe?"

"And bring it to me."

Steal? Bartholomew wanted him to steal something? Matt had never stolen anything in his life. Pa would tan his hide six ways to Sunday if—

"You scared?"

"No, I am not scared." And he wasn't. It was just a line he'd never crossed before…

Bartholomew smiled and leaned back on the wall. "Then let's see what you got."

Miffed at all but being called a coward, Matt stomped off toward the mercantile, just two stores away. He could do this. He'd show that big mouth Bartholomew G. Branson what a McCain was made of.

He shoved open the mercantile's door and then just kinda froze. His pa was standing over by the counter going over a list with Miss Gracie and a clerk. There was nobody watching the candy counter. It would be a snap to swipe something. He eased in quietly and meandered over to the jars full of colorful sweets.

He was no coward.

But as he watched his pa, he recalled him sitting by Ma's bed. Night after night. And the way he'd struggled to keep the farm from failing—yet, he'd never failed to make time for the Lord…and Matt. He was a good man.

So good, there were days Matt wanted to rage at his father to do just one thing less than perfect. A pointless sense of frustration roiled in his chest, but here and now was not the time to deal with it.

HE WALKED BACK OUTSIDE to Bartholomew. The boy pushed off the wall, grinning like a badger. "You get it?"

"Yeah. You didn't tell me what you wanted, so I got you this." He ripped the whip in half and handed off a piece.

Bartholomew's eyes widened with delight, then fear. "Say, we better get out of here."

"I didn't steal that candy. I bought it. With money I earned. I don't have any reason to run." Matt tapped the brim of his hat and turned back for the store.

Noble rested his hands on his hips and surveyed the area where Gracie and her husband had parked their wagon. It was one of those peddler's wagons, or what his granny would have called a medicine wagon. It was parked down in a wide, flat draw between a short, rocky mesa and a cut bank. A creek gurgled by, creating a nice, calming sound.

"Good spot. You're sheltered from the wind. You have water." He nodded. "It's not bad, but I should look around the land a little before we decide to build anything here." He kicked at the ground, covered in dry, golden prairie grass, eyed the cut bank a hundred yards away. "This area could flood now and again."

Gracie climbed down from the McCains' wagon and arched into a deep stretch. "I came out here four or five days after the blizzard. You couldn't see anything from the butte up there except the stove pipe. The whole wagon was buried in a drift."

"So, the draw catches the snow, huh?"

"On this side, that's for certain. The bank over there was bare."

Matt, who had dismounted from Gracie's horse Cyrus, tied the reins around a wagon wheel and smirked at her little home. "You lived in this? It's no bigger than our hen house."

"There's more room than you think. Take a look."

The living accommodations pulled Noble's mind back from the land for a moment. "Matt and I can pitch a tarp and sleep outside till we get a shelter built."

"That's nonsense. It's cold. The weather is unpredictable. We can all sleep in there. There are two beds."

Noble was shocked. "In there?"

"My husband Melvin was—"

Her sudden pause made Noble curious what she started to say but knew he wasn't at liberty to ask. Yet. So, he left her to choose the words she wanted to use.

"A clever fellow. He was very good with puzzles. The wagon is full of little hidden drawers and shelves. One bed folds out from a table."

"Oh. Well, I guess that will be alright for a while."

"And it's warm. Melvin made sure the walls and the floor are insulated."

"Yeah, Pa." Matt poked his head outside. "It is nice. Cozy."

For some reason the word made Noble take a step back. He didn't need to be cozy with the lady who was his business partner. The quick, little, *awkward* kiss he'd laid on her at the wedding was sticking in his mind for some reason.

He cleared his throat and climbed the butte behind the

wagon, only about twenty feet high. But from up here, he could see miles of flat terrain, interrupted here and there by a gently rolling hill. Lots of fine, empty land for farming. The creek snaked through it. "This is good acreage, Gracie. Melvin picked you a good spot. Just wish it had a little timber on it."

"It does," she called up. "Not much. A cluster of walnuts on the creek, oh, about a half-mile north."

"It would be nice to build a real barn and cabin. Not out of sod."

Gracie shook her body, as if the idea gave her the shivers. "I've read stories about those. Dirt falling into your food from the ceiling, rattlesnakes nesting in your walls. No thank you."

"Might not have any choice."

She chucked a finger at the wagon. "It's warm, it's dry, the beds are soft, and it's been my home for seven years. It can go another seven if need be." Noble studied her for a moment. She frowned at him. "You look perplexed."

"Just occurred to me all the little things I don't know about you. How old you are. Where you're from. Who your parents are. What did your husband do for a living?"

She kicked a rock on the ground and shrugged. "Guess we'll have time to talk."

"Yeah, I guess we will." He felt like he'd stumbled on to something awkward, so he changed the subject. He pointed at the side of her wagon. "What did it used to say?"

The wagon looked as if Gracie or someone had made an attempt to sand off its messages. A few faded, peeling letters remained randomly, but only in the very center. "Me..v… ole…tab…lix…"

"My husband was a salesman. He sold mostly…medicinal items."

Noble walked down to the wagon as he digested this information, dirt tumbling down in front of him. Gracie had hesitated and chosen her words carefully. He wondered about the details of her husband's profession. "You don't sound like it was —"

"We had happy customers and sometimes not-so-happy customers. Not every medicine we sold helped every person."

"Medicines are like that." He looked again at the side of the wagon. Someone had made a serious effort to erase the name Erstwhile. "Did he do this or did you?"

"The both of us. Melvin was retiring so we erased his name, hoping to avoid any of the unhappy customers."

This seemed a little much to Noble. Unless… "There a lot?"

"A few."

Well, Noble figured he couldn't blame a man for wanting to retire in peace. "You ever lived on a farm?"

She sighed and faced him directly. "I ran away from home when I was sixteen. My father was wealthy and spoiled me. I didn't even iron my own petticoats. I was with a theater troupe for several years. Then Melvin and I married and lived in this wagon. We moved from town to town buying or bartering for almost everything we needed. I can do a little cooking on our stove and I can…" She looked heavenward as if trying to recall just what her skills were. "That's about it. I've never milked a cow, planted a garden, ground flour or whatever people do on farms."

Noble tried to hold his face still. A good farm hand would have been too much to ask for, he supposed. "Mrs. Thompson had that on you then."

"Most of the women in Last Chance have a great many skills I do not have."

Matt chuckled as he clomped down the wagon's stairs. "Yeah, but they can't pull money out of their ears."

GRACIE MANAGED to pull together a stew and the three of them took advantage of the mild fall weather to enjoy the meal outside. While she had busied herself with the cooking, Noble and Matt had ridden off to see some of the landmarks.

Now, seated around the cook fire, they talked of plans as Gracie served them each a bowl from the pot hanging over the flames.

"It's a good stand of trees," Noble said, taking the food from her.

Gracie tried to ignore the imaginary spark that jumped when their fingers touched. But it certainly dragged her back to the real spark that had happened in front of the judge. A most amazing thing. An awkward, even endearing peck full of electricity. She shook her head, puzzled by it.

"Should be enough wood there to handle at least a small barn. Maybe a cabin." He tasted the stew and nodded his approval. "This is good."

"Thank you." Was she also imagining the awkwardness between them now? Surely it would pass. They'd get used to each other. They had to.

Matt tried his. "Sure is."

"We won't starve," she said, settling on a box like the other two. "You might get tired of my limited menu, but we'll eat."

"Pa and I aren't too picky. Long as we don't have to do it."

Noble chuckled. "He's saying that you're a better cook than we are. Although I fry a mean egg."

"Then we'll need to purchase some chickens."

The three of them fell quiet for a few minutes, each, Gracie could tell, lost in their thoughts...and fears. Now that the deed was done and dark had fallen, Gracie was afraid again. Had she made a colossal mistake?

"So, you've never lived on a farm?" Matt asked, pushing the spoon around what sounded like an empty bowl.

"Nope. Closest thing I've ever done to milking a cow is trade a puppet show for a bottle of milk."

"Puppets? See, Pa. She's got all kinds of skills."

A flash of doubt crossed Noble's face and Gracie read it even in the dancing firelight. "She sure does. Son, why don't you go take a bath in the wagon before it gets too late."

"Would you like seconds before you go in?" Gracie asked.

"No, thank you, ma'am. It sure was good, though. Pa, you doing the dishes then?"

Gracie sucked in her bottom lip to control a smile. These two had grown accustomed to living without a woman and she was happy to see how long it lasted.

"Sure thing. Your turn tomorrow night."

When Matt left, Gracie decided she could eat another half-bowl. "I think I'll have a little more. You?"

"Yes, please. Best meal we've had in a while."

She served him, then herself, and settled back to finish. Noble casually tossed another small log on the fire, then glanced up at the wagon. "I should probably take some wood inside and make sure the stove is ready to go when we need it. This nice weather is a fluke."

"I've never seen anything like that blizzard. How fast it came in. They found bodies…" She shook off the memories of the parents they'd discovered down at the park. They'd been on their way to get their children from their schoolhouse.

"Kansas got hit hard, too. It was the last straw for us."

"It-it kind of scares of me to be out here. What if another storm like that comes in? We're out here alone. There's no wood stored up—"

"Don't talk yourself into a bad place. We'll be all right. In the morning, we'll move the wagon over there closer to the creek. You said the bank blocked a lot of the snow?"

"Yes."

"We'll build a shelter for the horses, stock up on wood…" He faded off with a troubled scowl.

"What's the matter?"

He huffed, a sound full of disgust, and set his bowl down. "Money. I don't come into this mar—*union* with more than a hundred dollars."

"I've got five hundred dollars. That will do everything we need, won't it?"

Her offer didn't affect the look on his face. "Not much of a partner. Letting the woman buy everything."

Now Gracie understood. She licked her spoon and set down her bowl as well. "Noble…" She'd didn't have the best bedside manner when it came to encouraging people. What could she say to him? "I'm better with children. You can show them a trick, do a puppet show, and then tell them no dream is beyond their reach and they'll believe you. Selling the fairy dust to a grown man is a different story." That was Melvin's job.

"Then don't try."

"No fairy dust. I will say this. We're both here with a chance to start over. I don't know if we've made the right choice but we—at least I am—committed to trying. You said you were a good farmer. You had some bad luck. Let's believe it's changed for the better now. I've got the funds and the land. You've got the know-how. Sounds fair to me."

He tapped his fingers together and sat silently staring into the fire. Gracie let him be to ruminate on things. Failure was always a difficult thing for a man to reconcile.

She was surprised by his question when he finally spoke. "You don't seem to miss your husband much. Wasn't a good marriage?"

"I met Melvin when I was nineteen. He was handsome and flashy. Had a gift for gab. That man, he could sell a bottomless bucket to sailors on a sinking ship. And then I realized one day I was like…like the moon orbiting the earth. I was there for him. I served a purpose, but he was as mindful of me as a man is of his shadow." *And I was so lonely.* "When he left with the hunting group, I was glad. For the first time in years, I was alone…and not because I was being ignored." Gracie cleared her throat, surprised at herself. "That probably doesn't make any sense. I can't explain it."

She looked across the fire at Noble. The scowl had left and now he stared at her with tenderness. "I'm sorry. I had a good marriage. I can't imagine…"

"You still miss your wife?"

He swallowed. "With every breath I take."

"Pa," Matt hollered from the wagon. "Miss Gracie. There's water in the basin still. Either one of you want a bath?"

Gracie's eyes widened at the same time as Noble's. "How are we going to do this?" she asked, referring to more than the bathing situation. How had they not thought this through?

He scratched his neck and wagged his head. "We'll just have to figure it out."

"Well, uh, why don't you wash up and I'll do the dishes."

"You cooked."

"But if I want to bathe, Matt will have to come outside and it's too cool now."

Noble eyed the wagon with suspicion. "Mighty tiny quarters. I'd like to get a cabin built before the weather sets in, but that's asking a lot."

Gracie rubbed her arms against the chill that was settling in for the night and repeated, "We'll just have to figure it out."

Noble eyed the interior of the little hen house on wheels with resignation. He was six foot four. The hair on his head brushed the ceiling. And the bed Gracie had suggested, the one at the back of the wagon, was the width of the wagon. Only six feet. The space between the stove, counter, and a few cabinets on the right and a little bench on the left was a hair over a foot. Worse, they'd stacked a couple of barrels of flour, sugar, and coffee on the counters and beneath the bench. It was going to be tight.

Matt was sitting up on the bed, staring back at him. "Tiny, isn't it? You aren't going to be able to stretch out up here."

Noble sighed. "We'll figure it out." Matt had left the water on the stove. They hadn't built a fire in the little cook stove, so it was cold, but not as cold as creek water, he reminded himself. He took off his shirt and began a simple bath, thinking of ways to encourage them. "It might be cramped but we won't be in here much."

Truth, for sure. Starting a farm from scratch. The tasks and chores whirled in his head. They'd build what they could in the winter, starting with a run-in shelter that they could add onto and make a barn, then buy some livestock, get to farming in the spring. Maybe somewhere in all that they'd start a cabin.

Matt was scrunched up in the corner of the bed, a lamp burning beside him, the Bible open on his lap. "Listen to this, Pa. 'Not that I speak in respect of want: for I have learned, in whatsoever state I am, therewith to be content. I know both how to be abased, and I know how to abound: every where and in all things, I am instructed both to be full and to be hungry, both to abound and to suffer need. I can do all things through Christ which strengtheneth me.'"

Noble hung his head, humbled by the scripture. "Yep. It can always be worse." Had been worse. He patted his shoulders and chest dry with a small hand towel and was reaching for his shirt when Gracie came in. "Oh, pardon me," she said, flustered and turning away. "I should have knocked."

"No, I'm done. Please come on in. And please tell me where you're sleeping. Thought you said there were two beds."

"There are."

She took two more steps in and Noble backed up two

steps to give her room. As he did, he caught the woody scent of a cook fire still clinging to her, and of oatmeal soap, and something sweeter. The scent of a woman. He thought again of their brief kiss, puzzled that it stayed with him.

"Right here." She pointed at the little bench with a couple of pillows and a quilt on it. She reached down and pulled the front face up, hesitating so Noble could back all the way up to Matt. When she folded up the board, two legs extended down. Then she grabbed one of the pillows, which turned out to be a thin, rolled up mattress. She snapped it open and spread it out on the bench. "Voila."

Now the aisle between both sides of the wagon was down to less than a foot. This was a heck of a thing they'd gotten themselves into, but he smiled as encouragingly as he could. "Clever."

Gracie's face fell and her gaze ricocheted around the wagon.

"Something the matter?"

"I—I, well, I didn't think ahead. I guess I'll sleep in my dress."

"Oh." Noble, too, looked around the wagon. Crowded and lacking in any privacy whatsoever. Then he noticed the curtain near the bed Matt was occupying, tied back out of the way. A privacy screen. She'd given up her bed for the two of them. "Here, why don't we do this. You sleep up there. That way you can pull the curtain. Matt, you sleep down here on the floor. Bring your quilt." The boy jumped down, blanket in hand.

"No, no," Gracie protested. "We can do something different tomorrow."

"No, I insist." Noble gently clutched her shoulders and attempted to switch places with her but the space was so tight she had to press up against him to make the transition.

"Oh, really you don't—"

Curves and warmth did not go unnoticed in Noble's

stressed, male brain, but once they'd managed the transition, he stepped back. "This will work better." He cleared his throat and reached for Matt. "Here, just step on the edge of the bed and come on."

Gracie's cheeks had turned a pretty shade of pink. She licked her lips and smoothed down her skirt. "All right. All right. Matt, there is an extra mattress under the bench." She looked lost for a moment, but then climbed up into the bed, and released the curtain.

Noble touched his chest and wondered at his heartbeat. A little too fast over nothing. To ground himself, he fixed firmly in his mind pictures of Jessie as he crawled onto the bench-bed contraption. Jessie holding Matt when he was born. Jessie smiling as she opened some little Christmas present.

He stretched out, unfolded the blanket over him, glad the narrow bed accommodated his long frame. "You all right down there, Matt?"

"Fine. Thank you, Miss Gracie."

"Oh, just glad we worked it out."

Noble lay still and listened to the sounds in their new *home*. It took Matt a minute to settle. Then he whispered his prayers. Noble heard a few things, something about getting along, blessing the new home, and a new saddle? Then the boy fell silent.

Behind the curtain, he heard the soft rustle of clothing and the accompanying gentle grunt as Gracie strained to remove her dress in the confined area. A picture of her in her shift came to him and he rolled over on his side.

Jessie. Jessie riding her favorite pinto across the farm, long, black hair flying free in the wind. Jessie walking behind the plow, laughing and planting corn, her feet bare and dirty in the freshly turned Kansas soil.

Jessie…

I miss her, Lord. I always will. But will I always be this miserable without her?

5

Noble had relocated with only the most basic necessities. Now, leaning on his wagon, studying Gracie's tiny, little, henhouse sized wagon, he thought of so many things he wished he'd held back from the bank.

He was an honorable man, though, and he'd owed a debt. He'd given the First Bank of Atchison as much as he could afford, plus some. He massaged his neck, surprised at the tension there. What precious little he had brought was going to push the space in the tiny home to the limit.

Sighing, he pulled the butter churn from the wagon and walked it over to Gracie, who was tugging on her coat. The day had turned cold, but at least it wasn't windy. "Have you ever made butter?" he asked.

She eyed the churn skeptically. "No. We always traded for it."

"Hmm." He set it on the ground between them. "What about bread?"

"On occasion I have managed a loaf."

"Well, Matt and I will finish unloading the wagon. Then I'll show you how to use this. And while he and I are out cutting timber, maybe you could manage biscuits, butter, and something for dinner?"

She laid her hand on the plunger. "I can come up with something, I'm sure."

"All right."

She'd cooked a good stew last night, but Matt and Noble had offered plenty of help and pointers. The woman could pull a nickel out of man's ear but she'd sliced vegetables like she'd never handled a knife before. Turning her into a farm hand was going to be a little more of a challenge than he'd planned.

But they'd figure it out.

AN HOUR LATER, Gracie stood on the wagon's steps and waved as Noble and Matt disappeared over the butte in their wagon. And the silence around her descended like a shroud. The plains of Nebraska were wild and lonely. She listened for a moment, amazed by the autumn quiet. So many years spent camping on the edge of towns, behind saloons, or in groups of wanderers. She'd never been this…isolated.

"Well, this isn't getting any butter churned." She spun and eyed the tall, wooden churn like it was an enemy. Noble had helped her fill it with the heavy cream they'd purchased in town, and then he'd explained the process. Gracie was confident she had a handle on it and had insisted she do the work inside. Noble had smiled patiently and promised her within a few minutes, she'd be happy the churn was outside.

She currently still disagreed with this idea, but reached for the plunger and began the tedious work of making butter. In five minutes, her shoulders were aching, and she'd already switched arms three times. Into the process ten minutes, she'd taken three breaks.

"And I'm supposed to do this for an hour?" Her arms hurt. Her neck and shoulders were complaining. Even her hands ached. The constant up and down movement of the plunger, broken intermittently by a twist or a spin, was a slow form of death. She wiped her brow, startled by the beads of sweat, and sent her gaze out to the prairie. "He warned me. And, yes, I'm glad I'm out here."

Her back and arms screaming, eventually the butter appeared. Gracie chuckled faintly. "Well, look at that," she said, gazing down into the churn. "I made butter." And once she drained off the buttermilk, she'd make biscuits. "I am a pioneer woman."

She didn't know she had it in her. This labor was a lot harder than picking pockets and scamming innocent citizens…but it was clean work. Melvin had said over and over that what they did wasn't so bad. But now, looking at the fruits of her labor, she felt…light. After every show with Melvin, an uncomfortable feeling used to dog her for days—tweaking and pinching like a tight corset.

Next, using two wooden paddles, she scooped the butter from the churn and attempted shaping it into a three-pound square. Her hands, used to quick, delicate maneuvers, got the idea quickly and soon the butter had a nice, finished shape.

That chore accomplished, Gracie made the biscuits and popped them in the oven. Then she looked around the tiny living space, crowded and crammed with a minimal number of supplies. *What next?*

To help her think, she pulled a deck of cards from one of the small drawers and began shuffling them with skill and precision. Keeping her fingers limber had put food on their table more than a few times—

She stopped herself and looked down at her hands holding the cards. "I don't need to do this anymore. Do I?"

Did she?

I'm legitimate now. I've gone straight.

Before she could finish deliberating, the rattle of the wagon interrupted her ruminating. She shoved the cards back into their home and hurried outside.

"Back so soon?" she asked as Noble pulled the horses to a stop. A glance at the back of the wagon showed an impressive stack of logs. "My, you have been busy."

He locked the brake and jumped down, stretching stiffly, as if his joints ached. "It was a good stand and Matt and I are pretty fast at felling trees."

Matt came around and joined his father. "It'll get us started on a run-in."

"You don't happen to have dinner ready early, do you?"

"No, I've just got—" she gasped. *The biscuits!*

She whirled and ran back inside, swiped the potholder from the counter, and flung open the little oven. "No, no, no," she cried as she pulled out the biscuits. Not burnt black but they were only a shade or two from it. Disgusted, she set them down. *How could you be so addle-brained, Gracie?*

"Ah, that's all right, Miss Gracie," Matt said magnanimously. "They aren't too bad." He had his rifle in his hand and shrugged. "I'm gonna see if I can scare up a couple of pheasants to go with them."

Gracie tilted her head and smiled at the boy. "Takes a lot to make you complain, doesn't it?"

"Well, burnt biscuits isn't the worst it can be."

No, she supposed it wasn't. Still, she appreciated his patience. Melvin would have quietly berated her for a week.

"Tell you what. You come back with anything for supper and I'll teach you a trick."

His face lit up. "Every jack rabbit and pheasant out there better worry."

He skedaddled and Gracie leaned her hip on the counter. Annoyed with her lack of attention, she picked up a biscuit and dropped it. It sounded like a rock.

"Maybe you did us a favor."

She glanced up at Noble standing in the doorway. She was ready to defend herself, but he was smiling, too. "I've burned some food in my lifetime. It happens."

"I'll try not to make a habit of it."

"That would be appreciated." He chuckled then added, "Matt'll bring something back for supper. Can I get you to help me unload these logs?"

Gracie tensed and ran her fingertips over her thumbs. "Of course."

"You don't sound so sure."

"No, I'll gladly help." Her hands were valuable. She'd learned to protect them. "It's just that my hands..."

"You can wear Matt's gloves."

"All right."

As it turned out, hurting her hands was a fair concern. The logs were heavy, she wasn't used to such physical labor, and her skirt was a true hindrance. Twice she nearly tripped over the hem as she helped lift and then stack the logs.

Taking the last one out of the wagon, she held tight to her end as Noble lifted his and climbed from the back. Gracie had worked up a sweat and was more tired than she'd ever been in her life. Her arms felt like noodles. Pioneering was hard.

She and Noble side-stepped over to the stack of logs and as she was laying her end down, the lumber rolled. Pain seared her fingertips, and she snatched her hand free with a yelp, leaving the glove behind.

Gracie cursed angrily—a mild oath, but Noble's eyes widened into full moons as she waved the stinging fingers in the air, then clutched them to her chest. She groaned in a deep, breathy way, and then looked up at him.

"Are you all right?"

She heard the disapproval in his voice, though he seemed to be trying to keep his face inscrutable. Gracie flexed her fingers. The pain was fading. Everything bent like it should. "I'm sorry. I'm fond of my fingers."

He relaxed a little. "I guess if anything will make a body cuss, it's smashing a finger."

But Gracie knew Noble wouldn't have cussed. Was there anything on the planet that could make him lose his temper enough to release expletives? She doubted it. "My hands, they've kept me fed."

His brow dipped. "Don't most people's?"

"Yes. No, I mean…" She thought a demonstration was in order and it would test her agility. She walked toward Noble and tripped on her hem. He caught her and she backed away. "Sometimes I can be so clumsy." She held out her hand and showed him a tiny pocketknife. "If that's all you have in your pocket, you *are* broke."

Noble gasped and checked his pocket, turning it out. Then an odd expression crossed his handsome, chiseled face. Mistrust. Disappointment. Gracie knew the look well. And she was sorry she'd shown him her skills.

"You're a thief."

Gracie felt as if he'd slapped her. The word sounded so ugly when he said it. "I was." She didn't like being looked down upon, whether it was justified or not. At least Melvin had appreciated her skills. "I stole to survive. Not anymore." Pastor Collins' watch had been the first thing she'd lifted in a while and she'd done it for pure meanness. Now, suddenly, the move felt petty.

Noble made a sucking sound with his teeth and turned away. He took a few steps, rubbing his stubbly jaw. "Is it over?" He rested his hands on his hips and rounded on her. "Being in a business deal with a thief isn't something I'm real comfortable with."

"I would never—I *will* never steal from you. I've gone straight."

He cocked his head to one side. "What about other people?"

"I don't know if other people have gone straight or not."

The joke fell flat. Noble had this look in his eyes like he'd figured something out. Gracie felt vaguely as if he was catching on to her subtle use of words. But she wouldn't be cornered or promise something she wasn't ready to give ground on. "It was a skill I only used when I had to." Melvin had also taught her to speak with obscurity. Use words to create a rabbit trail, make people forget the specific answer they needed. "This farm, our arrangement, you and Matt— that's what I'm committed to now. Stealing isn't necessary."

Noble held her gaze. Oh, she could see the wheels turning behind his piercing dark eyes. "And it won't be. Right?"

She smiled. "I have all the confidence in our venture. It won't be necessary."

6

"Miss Gracie?"

Gracie heard a voice calling her from far away. Far out in a field of wheat, beautiful, golden…dancing joyously with the wind.

"Miss Gracie?"

Her eyes fluttered open. Matt. Matt was calling her. She reached over and pulled the curtain back enough to see his smiling, tanned face.

"Good morning, Miss Gracie."

"Morning." The smell of bacon rushed at her. She looked past the boy to Noble, hunched over their little cooking stove, tending to bacon in the pan. Despite her misgivings about this arrangement, he was a nice sight in the morning. Tall, lean, muscular.

Honest to a fault.

"Pa's almost got breakfast ready. We'll eat and then get out of your way so you can dress for church."

"Church?"

Noble paused poking at the bacon, then resumed, but slower, listening. Gracie tapped Matt on the nose. "Church sounds like a wonderful idea."

GRACIE COULDN'T RECALL the last time she'd actually been inside a church. As the wagon approached the building, it's prim, white steeple pointing to the sapphire sky, she thought back to a tent revival. Dodge City, maybe?

She'd wandered in just to get out of the rain. And the pastor had said such nice things about Jesus. How much He loved her. So much He'd died for her. And today was the day of decision. Gracie remembered a stirring in her soul, her heart racing, muscles tensing to move her off the bench, carry her down that long aisle—

And Melvin had clutched her shoulder, demanded she leave right then. Leave the revival, leave Dodge. Seconds ahead of an irate customer.

Noble tugged on the reins, slowing the team down from a trot to a walk. "It's church, not an execution."

She glanced over, surprised to find him watching her. "Oh, I was just remembering…Melvin." She shrugged her shoulders against the chill and the memory.

Thankfully, Noble didn't pursue it and proceeded to park the wagon next to a cottonwood tree. Church, it seemed, had not started yet. At least a dozen folks were standing outside the door, bundled up in coats, but chatting as if it were a balmy summer day. Noble offered his arm to Gracie. A little surprised, she accepted it and the three of them trekked toward the group.

His arm felt surprisingly comfortable, natural beneath her fingers. But, of course, this was all for appearance's sake. No need to give legs to any rumors that might be swirling about their sudden union. What happened out at her farm was hers and Noble's business. Why they had married with the judge and not Pastor Collins was their business.

They approached the crowd and Heather Barnes turned. A pretty girl with blonde hair and blue eyes to match her dress, she was a widow who had taken the death of her husband hard. Smiling now, she offered her hand first to Gracie.

"It's nice to see you. I'd heard you finally got on the mail-order groom train." The woman flicked a curious glance up at Noble. "Though you certainly kept it a secret. We were astonished to hear of your wedding."

Gracie thought her face might crack with the thin, fake smile pasted on it. As she'd suspected, the town's rumor mill was going. Every town had one. "Yes. This is Noble McCain. His son Matt. This is Heather Barnes, the town midwife."

"Gentlemen. Lovely to meet you." They shook hands then Heather brought her gaze back to Gracie. "Mrs. Erstwhile here was a tad hesitant about the plan to find a mail order husband." She reached out and squeezed Gracie's hand. "And I'm sure it wasn't an easy decision, but life moves on."

Who was she trying to convince? Gracie wondered. The sadness in her voice spoke volumes. The tensed muscles in Noble's arm expressed his feelings, as well. For these two, the loss of their spouses had been a bitter pill. Gracie only felt guilty that she didn't miss Melvin more.

She felt her smile falter but forced it back, bigger and brighter. "Yes. Moving on. We have all kinds of plans, that's for sure."

"Wonderful. Wonderful."

Before Gracie could say anything else, a slender, sultry blonde with icy blue eyes and an intense stare nudged through the crowd to stand beside Heather. Gracie's stomach curdled. Jillian Weatherspoon had taken a dislike to her for no apparent reason. And while she was civil about it, she reminded Gracie of a cat on the hunt, acting bored to lull the mouse into a false sense of security. Only, Gracie was not fooled.

"Well, well, well, if it isn't our mysterious little Gracie Erstwhile," she dripped out in her Southern honey accent.

"Oh, um," Gracie snapped her fingers. "Janice, right?"

The girl's face tightened up like a banjo string, but she held on to her smile. "Jillian. Jillian Weatherspoon. And this handsome thing must be your new husband." She unabashedly surveyed Noble from head to toe.

"Yes. Noble this is Josie—I mean, Jillian Weatherspoon. She does…something in town."

Daggers flew out of Jillian's eyes. Heather must have seen them. "Well, if you'll excuse me, I'm going inside. I'll see all of you later. Mr. McCain, Matt, so nice to have met you."

Father and son nodded goodbye. "Ma'am," Noble said.

Jillian then offered her hand to Noble who responded politely but blandly, Gracie thought. "My daddy owns the feed and seed in Last Chance. I'm sure I'll be seeing you soon."

"I'm sure." He wiped his hand nervously on his thigh. Grace saw the motion. She didn't think Jillian did, who was too busy batting her eyelashes at the tall man. "We've just got three horses," he explained, "but they'll be in need of grain."

"Oh, Noble," Gracie snapped her fingers, "Jocelyn's father is also a livestock trader and we're going to want to buy stock soon."

Jillian's eyes narrowed down to slivers but that smile stayed in perfect position. "Jillian. It's Jillian," she enunciated softly, then turned again to Noble. "So, what are y'all doing for accommodations? Are you living in that precious little wagon Mrs. Erstwhile and her husband—her first husband—brought into town? I thought it was positively adorable. Such an adventurous way to live. And I know the hotel must be getting expensive."

"We're getting by comfortably in the wagon," Noble said.

"It's quite cozy." Gracie moved forward just a hair. "And it's Mrs. McCain now, Lillian."

Gracie and Jillian locked gazes like two spitting cats. Bless his heart, Matt cleared his throat and motioned toward the door. "Excuse me, ladies, but folks are going in."

"Oh, yes, of course." Gracie took a step forward. "Why don't you sit with us, Jocelyn?" She placed a hand on Jillians' shoulder, attempted to nudge her to join them, but stumbled over the hem of her dress. Jillian, out of human reflex, caught her, but what a glare followed the action.

"Oh, I'm sorry." Gracie said, backing off. "So clumsy of me."

"Yes, it was." Jillian moved off a step as well. "I have to sit with my parents. Mr. McCain, young Matt, lovely to have met you."

Gracie flashed her a big, warm, departing grin.

"Son, go inside and get a seat. Miss Gracie and I will be right there."

Matt regarded them both with bewilderment, but nodded and went inside. Noble gave the surrounding parishioners time to disappear inside the door as well. Gracie didn't know what she'd done, but she felt as if a thunderstorm was coming her way.

Noble didn't disappoint. "I don't know what that was all about, but give it back," he said quietly through clenched teeth.

"Give what back?"

He looked around and then moved closer. His eyes, a dark chocolate now, burned with anger. "You said you wouldn't do that anymore. March right in there and give it back."

"What?"

"I don't know *what*, but I know you took something from that girl. And you will give it back or I will turn you over my knee."

Gracie gasped indignantly and backed up. "You wouldn't dare."

"Do you want to test me?"

Did she? Gracie could read people. Well. And what she saw now was a man who wanted to teach her a lesson. How, she wasn't sure, and that was where her confidence wavered. Would he spank her right here? Knowing his black-and-white idea of honesty, he just might.

But he sagged. "No, I would never hit a woman. Even you."

Gracie strangled a howl of anger, but couldn't stop the sneer on her lips. "Fine." She held up her hand and a dainty, little bracelet dangled from her fingers. "But it serves her right, flirting with a married man. She's a trollop."

Noble sucked in his cheeks like he was holding back a flood of arguments. Finally, he said, "You are in no position to judge anyone."

Gracie deflated with the truth. She curled her fingers around the bracelet. Without another word she marched into the church, scanned the heads, saw the blonde curls she was looking and headed for them.

"Lillian, I mean Jillian, you dropped this outside." Gracie, with flair, dangled the bracelet in front of the girl.

Jillian's eyes widened and then they narrowed again with suspicion. Before she could respond, a grizzled old man with a magnificent beard, leaned over, eyes glowing with delight. "Why, that is most kind of you, Miss Erstwhile. Thank you."

"Yes. Thank you," Jillian repeated. "Only, it's Mrs. McCain now, Daddy."

"Oh. Well, thank you, Mrs. McCain."

"Certainly. It's delicate, Joss—I mean, Jillian. You should be careful with it."

Gracie smiled at the woman and her father, and strode back toward Noble and Matt. While she had done the right thing—supposedly—she was seething with anger and humiliation. At least Melvin had never berated her like a child.

7

So many people at church wanted to meet the newest mail-order groom in town, it was easy for Gracie to slip away. Muttering to herself and ruminating on thoughts of leaving this dusty, two-bit town, she stomped down to the depot. She had all her money with her. She could take the boat across the river and disappear some place—any place—the self-righteous Noble McCain was not.

Spank her, would he?

Fuming, she dropped down on the bench and bounced her knee like she was waiting on Santa. Only she wasn't expecting gifts. Her blood was boiling. Noble had made her feel about two feet tall. *Well, I'm so sorry I'm not perfect like you, Noble.*

Frustrated, unexpectedly fighting tears, she dropped her head into her hands to think.

"Miss Gracie?"

Matt. God love him, he'd followed her. At the moment, she didn't want his or anyone's company, but he was here. Sighing, she sat back up and smiled at the boy, the cool breeze ruffling black strands of hair around his face in the shadow of his hat. Handsome. Just like his father.

He tucked his hands inside his coat pocket and dropped onto the bench beside her. "You all right? You left church in a huff."

"Was it obvious?"

"Yeah."

"I did something your pa didn't appreciate. He treated me like a child over it. I'm not used to that."

Matt puttered his lips and nodded. "That's Pa. So..." He looked around. "You leaving?"

"I sure was thinking about it."

"Can I go with you?"

"What? Why would you want to do that?"

He hunched his shoulders. "There's nothing to this town. Pa's never gonna let me grow up. He's right all the time about everything."

"He is that."

"Makes me want to haul off and just..."

"Strangle him?"

"Yeah...You know, if you're leaving, I've got a little money saved up. Not much. Just twenty dollars, but I'd give it to you. You...you need somebody to look after you."

Gracie bit her bottom lip to keep her mouth from falling open. If the boy only knew Gracie's skill set. Regardless, Matt's dissatisfaction with things here—probably teenage angst—shocked her.

Or maybe, as much as he wanted to be a man, he also just missed his mother. "How did your mother pass?"

"Doc said Cholera. Before we knew what was happening, she was gone."

"Least you had her for a little while. My mother died when I was very young. I don't even remember her. Except for a picture of her over our fireplace."

"What about your pa?"

"He's doing all right. Lives in Massachusetts. Last I'd heard, he'd remarried."

"You-you don't talk to him?"

"We had a fight when I was sixteen and I ran away. Like you, I was champing at the bit to get out on my own, see the world, experience adventure..."

"Did you? Did you do all those things?"

"Mostly, I guess."

"When was the last time you talked to your pa?"

"The night I left."

"Holy sm—" He hung his head. "That's been a long time?"

"Eleven years." Gracie snugged her coat tighter, a chill sinking into more than her bones. "I write him every now and then to let him know I'm alive, but I don't give him a return address."

"Why do you do that? He's probably not still mad after all these years."

How could Gracie explain to a boy so eager to get out on his own what a failure she felt like? Her father had tried to warn her she was ill prepared for a hard, cold, selfish world.

"Well, that was pretty dang rude."

Both Matt and Gracie froze over the anger in Noble's voice. Slowly, they looked up and flinched at the thunder in his expression. Moving like condemned men, they rose as he stomped up to them.

"I could take you both over my knee for abandoning me

like that with all those strangers." He cut his eyes at Gracie. "Especially with Jillian."

"Don't yell at her, Pa." Matt inched in front of Gracie. "She left because you embarrassed her—"

"Matt, I can—"

"How did I embarrass her? How did I embarrass you?"

"We're both past being threatened with whuppins."

"No, you're not."

"I am so."

"Boys, boys." Gracie squeezed her hands between them and shoved them apart. "Both of you need to stop this."

"He acts like he's the only adult here."

"I am."

"An adult wouldn't have lost our farm."

"Matt," Gracie snapped. "Stop. You should show your father more respect than this."

"When he deserves it."

As the two went back and forth with these bitter barbs Gracie fished in her reticule for an instrument to silence them. She pulled a small, round tube of paper from her purse. "Stop this fussing right now. Here." She grabbed Matt's hand. "Put your finger in there."

"What?"

"Put your finger there. Right here." She pointed at the opening.

"I don't think—" Noble started to object, but Gracie silenced him with a glare. Matt put his finger in the tube. Gracie took Noble's hand and he hesitantly allowed her to guide his finger into the paper tube as well.

"There." She dropped their hands and stepped back.

"This isn't f—" Noble stopped as he tugged on the paper and it didn't release his finger.

Matt tugged and tugged again, harder. "Hey, what's going on here?"

Both men tugged and tugged but the trap held tight.

Noble stopped moving and leveled a deadly scowl on Gracie. "This another one of your tricks?"

"Oh, that's no trick."

"And it's none too funny," Matt complained, still trying to tug his finger free.

Gracie waited until they both stilled and looked at her with vexed expressions. "Now that I have your attention. Matt, show your father respect. He's working hard to take care of you." She softened her voice. "Be glad that you still have him." Then she slowly slid her gaze up to meet Noble's. "And you. Maybe what I did back there—No, scratch that. I told you stealing wouldn't be necessary anymore. I never said I wouldn't do it."

He sucked in a breath. Gracie could feel the anger emanating from him like the breeze off Galveston Bay. "I knew you were playing some kind of game with your words."

"I was. Now, no more games. No more stealing. Including from other people. I quit. I give you my good word. I'm sorry for…well, lying, sort of."

With that, she stepped away a few feet and stared off over the Platte, watching the breeze ripple across the water, giving the boys time to think. She'd run from the church feeling so dejected, angry, and truthfully, embarrassed. She didn't like feeling shame and worse, didn't like that Noble had made her feel it.

Noble sighed heavily, shook his head. "I'm sorry. I apologize to both of you."

"Yeah." Matt tugged on the finger trap. "I'm sorry, too, Pa."

"Honesty is important to me, Gracie. You let me down, but I didn't handle it right. I've got no excuse for threatening to spank you. Never have and never will hit a woman."

Wait? What? She'd let *him* down? The idea was so novel it nearly drowned out his apology. The only way she'd ever let

Melvin down was if she missed a cue or forgot a line. Noble McCain was disappointed that she was a liar and a thief. He was a man she was having a terrible time understanding. He thought so differently from her. "Apology accepted."

He and Matt nodded and then raised their captive fingers, expressions full of hope. Chuckling, Gracie pushed their hands toward one another and released them, first Matt then Noble. Noble took the little trap from her and turned it this way and that, as if looking for its power.

Then he gave it back to her. "You are full of surprises."

His gaze seemed to probe too deeply, and she looked away.

8

Noble led their two horses into the run-in they'd just finished and closed the rough-hewn gate. He slapped his hand on it and nodded with satisfaction. "A barn would be better, but this'll do."

Matt rested his hand on the gate as well. "Better than nothing. It's a good spot. The bank blocks a lot of the wind."

And the wind was picking up, Noble noted.

"Supper's ready, boys," Gracie called from the wagon.

The little hen-house-on-wheels, as Noble always thought of it, was a fine sanctuary on a cold, windy day. He and Matt entered and the warmth, the savory smells, and the pretty woman cooking at the stove was enough to brighten even the worst mood. Today, all her pretty blonde hair was braided atop her head, giving him a look at what a smooth, slender neck she—

He derided himself for even thinking about such things and peeled out of his coat.

They'd fallen into a routine finally, and he was glad to say the incident at church had been left behind. They were all treating each other with more respect and patience.

Just yesterday, Noble had jury-rigged Gracie's bed to fold up to the ceiling, making room for a little, low table. The three of them had managed, knee-to-knee, to share a meal. Crowded, tight, but he liked it. Before, they'd found any space they could to sit with a plate or bowl on their laps. It surprised him that Melvin had never bothered with a table for meals.

Gracie filled three plates with ham, red eye gravy, and biscuits and set them on the table. The three settled and she bowed her head. Noble grinned and followed suit. Gracie knew the routine, too. He blessed the food and they dug in.

"Matt, why don't we spend half the day tomorrow cutting some more timber, and then the other half riding our property lines and do some crop planning?"

"Okay with me."

"What does crop planning entail," Gracie asked, cutting off a piece of ham with her fork. "Simple as it sounds?"

"We look the land over, estimate the size of our fields, what we can plant where, and rotation options. We'll be able to figure how much seed to buy. What we'll need to grow for feed and for sale."

Noble was eager for spring. He missed the feel of the warm, dark earth in his hands, the satisfaction of watching his crops grow, and the good Lord blessing them.

"Oh, and when you go into town tomorrow," he rose and leaned over to the satchel he kept stored in the daytime on the far end of the bench. "I was wondering if you might put these in a safe deposit box." He pulled out a handful of papers and a small tin box and set them on the bench beside Gracie.

She lifted the top half of the first page so its heading was visible. Their marriage certificate. "Legal documents. Yes, I suppose we should keep these safe."

"The land claim is in there. Also got the bill of sale for my horse there, my marriage certificate, and the box has some sentimental doo-dads in it." His father's watch. His and Jessie's wedding rings. He glanced at Gracie's left hand. She saw him look.

"Excuse me, for a minute." Matt wiped his mouth and stood. "I'll be right back. Pa, did you leave, you know, anything in the…?"

"Left a whole Sears Catalog out there." They'd also managed to hastily construct an outhouse. It wasn't all that warm, but it was warmer than the way they had been addressing the nature calls.

Gracie seemed distracted and didn't notice the boy's departure. Noble picked up his plate, spun, and set it in the sink. "Who's turn on dishes?"

"Yours, I think," she said absently.

Again, Noble looked at her left hand. Not even a sign of a ring. "Did you, um, never wear a wedding ring?"

She extended the fingers on her left hand as if she had forgotten they were there. "A ring?" He could tell by the faraway look in her eyes that the question made her fall into a memory. But she answered with a simple, "He never bought me one."

For some reason, Noble doubted this answer. Had they been too poor, or the husband too distracted, to purchase one? Crying shame. He sopped up some gravy with his biscuit and changed the subject. "Where does this love of acting come from?"

She took several seconds to answer. "Acting always trans-ported me out of situations I found unpleasant. I could go anywhere, be anyone. If I did it well, the audience went with me."

"So, with you and Melvin, how did acting work into his—"

"It didn't," she said too quickly. "I was working with a small acting troupe when I met him. A few months later, when he asked me to marry him, I quit. I did try to talk him into creating his own troupe." She shrugged. "He wasn't interested."

"But you are. That's why you want to open a theater."

"Yes. Acting makes me feel like anything is possible."

Immediately he thought of the scripture *with God all things are possible* but kept it to himself. Something told him the Kingdom would call to Gracie someday, but there was a little softening still to do.

"What do you want to do? Perform like Sarah Bernhardt? Or do something else? Like your magic tricks?" He failed to keep the disdain from his voice with the last question.

"I want to perform. Especially the classics, like Shakespeare. He's magnificent."

"One evening you'll have to entertain Matt and me. Winter nights get long and boring, and I noticed you don't knit."

She laughed and said, "I noticed the same thing about you." He laughed at the joke, but it faded when she asked, "You read the Bible every night?"

"Pretty near. There's been more than one occasion when I came in from the field and was so tired, I fell asleep right in the middle of it, though."

She nodded and the conversation lagged. His eyes fell on the legal papers and he motioned to them. "You should add any of your important papers in there."

"Mine?"

"Sure. Posterity might care to see your first marriage certificate." He leaned forward, grinning. "Someday you might be the mysterious great grandmother that lived a wild and exciting life of legend and lore."

She smiled, but it was a little sad, he thought. "Maybe."

THE NEXT MORNING, Gracie waited until the wagon carrying Noble and Matt disappeared over the top of the butte. And then she waited another five minutes. Convinced they weren't returning, she lifted the corner of her mattress and pushed on a board. The other end popped up, revealing a secret compartment about nine inches long. She reached in and pulled out *her* legal documents.

The wanted poster with a poor likeness of her, accusing her of picking pockets in Virginia. True. Another alleging she'd participated in counterfeiting. Not true. And her marriage certificate. Marcus Julius Davenport and Gracelyn Leah Walker. Her and Melvin's real names. In the handful of years they'd spent together, how many times had they changed their names to avoid irate, even threatening customers and law enforcement officers? Ten? Fifteen?

Why had she kept this? Any of these papers could destroy whatever decent, legal life she wanted to have. She rose and went to the stove, intent on burning them, but stopped. The one piece of truth in this web of lies was her marriage certificate. And someday, maybe she would tell Noble everything. But not yet.

She burned the wanted posters and then readied for the cold ride to town.

9

———————

At a steady jog, Cyrus, Gracie's gelding, made town in just under an hour. Securing a safe deposit was quick and efficient, and, strangely, tucking her marriage certificate away for safe keeping made her feel better. It wasn't under foot to be accidentally discovered in the wagon. Instead, it would sit tight in the dark until who knew when?

Until she had the guts to tell Noble without that maddening fear of disappointing him. Again.

Noble, I lied about my name...Noble, I have been lying about my background...

It took Gracie a few moments to realize that in the traffic on the boardwalk, someone had fallen into step beside her.

Unfortunately, it turned out to be Jillian Weatherspoon, peering at Gracie with a bored house cat expression, as if she'd finally killed the mouse she'd been torturing.

"Good afternoon, Mrs. McCain," she said pointedly, as if doubting the name.

"Good afternoon…Miss Weatherspoon."

"How are things with you and your handsome new family?"

Gracie actually grimaced. Everything this woman said had some undertone. And while Gracie spent very little time chatting with anyone in town, she'd overheard enough to gather Jillian was presumptuous and flirtatious with every man under the age of fifty. And for whatever reason, she had developed a keen dislike for Gracie. Though Gracie knew she would deny it. So, did that mean she had drawn a target on her new husband?

"We are just fine. How are you and your parents?"

"Fine."

The women went several steps further in silence until Jillian asked, "What exactly did you say your husband, your first husband, did before y'all came to Last Chance?"

Gracie had been very careful with this answer, saying as little as possible as this whole mail-order groom plan had erupted around her. She'd sat in the back of the church the night Pastor Collins had pushed for it. She'd offered no opinions on the ads Heather had placed in the newspapers. She'd been the last widow in town to grab her handful of letters. And she'd sat on them for a month.

She'd kept her cards close to her vest, as Melvin would have said. Perhaps it was this very aloofness that drove Jillian to dislike Gracie. No reason to change things now. "My husband was in sales. Good day, Lillian." With that, Gracie turned abruptly and stepped into the mercantile.

• • •

GRACIE HAD no idea what would be useful or appreciated Christmas gifts for Noble and Matt, but as she wandered around the mercantile, she picked up some socks and gloves for them both, knives, some candy, and a dime novel for Matt. With these few items and an idea for a simple Christmas, she was strolling toward the counter when she noticed a little girl sitting in the back of the store near the stove.

A beautiful child of about five or six, with a full head of rebellious red curls, she sat in a wheelchair, entertaining herself rather listlessly with a doll. Gracie watched her for a minute and couldn't resist a chance to make her smile. She set the basket she was carrying on the counter and pulled out a pair of socks. Casually, she drifted over to the girl.

"Would your friend like to play with mine?" She raised her hands, covered with the socks, and began talking to the little girl, opening and closing her fingers. "My name is Cymbeline," she said in a deep and raspy voice. Then she raised her voice to a squeaky pitch. "And my name is Pericles. And we're having a terrible fight."

The little girl laughed and turned her doll around to face the socks. "What are you fighting about?" the doll asked by way of her owner.

"Ah, first," Cymbeline said, "You must tell us your name."

The little girl wiggled the doll. "I am Penelope."

"And what is your name?" Pericles asked the little girl.

"I'm Betsy."

"All right, Betsy," Pericles began, as Gracie lowered to her knees in front of the girl. "Cymbeline and I can't decide for the life of us what is the best candy in the world. Is it lollipops or jawbreakers?"

"Oh," the little girl's face went dark with the solemnity of the question, "Penelope and I know the answer to that one. It is lollipops."

"You're sure?" asked Cymbeline.

"Oh, quite sure," Betsy said.

"Like this maybe?" Slowly, Pericles disappeared behind Gracie's back and in a flash returned holding a lollipop. Betsy's face lit up as if it were already Christmas morning. "How did you do that?"

Not easily with these socks. Gracie extended the candy. "You can have this if it would be all right with your mother and father."

"Yes, it's fine." A young woman, not much older than Gracie, stepped out from behind the shelves. Her eyes were a little wet and Gracie hoped she hadn't over-stepped. Unsure if she was in trouble or not, she rose. "I hope it was all right."

"It was wonderful. You're very talented."

"Oh, it's nothing." She turned her sock puppets to the girl again. "Betsy," Pericles asked, "Do you like…" Gracie wracked her brain. What did she have in the reticule on her wrist? "Do you like whirligigs?"

"Sure. Yes." The girl nodded her head with enthusiastic abandon.

"All right, well, give us just a moment." Gracie turned her back on her little audience and pretended to be in a conference with the puppets. "There must be one in there," Cymbeline argued.

"I'm looking, I'm looking," she said.

In reality, Gracie had stripped off the socks and was rummaging through her purse. "Sometimes, Betsy, Pericles and Cymbeline get their magic mixed up and they mix me up. But let's see." *There must be something…* "They had to leave but they both informed me that you have a whirligig in your ear."

Betsy gasped and touched her ear. "No, I don't."

"Oh, I think you have something in your ear." Gracie spun back around, moved quickly and smoothly, and appeared to pluck her fake mustache from the girl's ear. "A mustache? What in the world?"

Betsy collapsed into laughter as Gracie pressed it over the

girl's lip. Betsy giggled so hard tears streamed from her eyes. "What do I look like, Mama? Do I look like a pirate?"

Her mother was laughing richly and joyously as well. "Oh, my, Betsy, you look like Black Beard himself."

Gracie glanced around and was astonished to see four other people had wandered up and appeared to be enjoying the show. Suddenly, Betsy's mother hugged Gracie, holding her in a death grip for a moment. "Thank you. Thank you. This is the most I've heard Betsy laugh in months."

"I'm so glad I could make her smile."

The woman stepped back, dabbing at her eyes. "I'm Ruth Johnson, by the way. Betsy is my daughter."

"I'm Gracie McCain." She couldn't take the pitiful look in the woman's eyes and swung her attention back to Betsy. "You take care of that mustache. Maybe next time Pericles and Cymbeline will have an eye patch for you."

Gracie backed herself away from the chuckling, smiling crowd, turned, and came face-to-face with Jillian. The woman's eyes glittered like a snake's, but Gracie had no time for her pettiness. "Excuse me."

Jillian didn't follow her, but Gracie could feel the stare scalding her backside. And it didn't dampen her mood one bit. Making Betsy laugh was the best thing that had happened to Gracie in months. In fact, the little impromptu show had only deepened her determination to open a theater one day. She would have acting classes, too, so that children like Betsy could get up out of their wheelchairs—if only in the world of pretend.

When Noble and Matt returned from a day of cutting timber and determining plots for crops, they entered the little medicine wagon dirty, dog-tired, and cold. But a couple of steaks and some potatoes frying on the stove…and a tiny

Christmas tree, all of about six inches high, brought them back to life.

"Well, look at that," Noble said, hanging his hat by the door and shrugging out of his coat. He motioned with his chin for Matt to notice it. Sitting in the window, the tree's root ball was wrapped in burlap, and a little, red ribbon zig-zagged around it. On the shelf over the window, Gracie had stored some presents wrapped in brown paper and tied with the same red ribbon.

She flipped a steak and shrugged. "It's a tiny tree. I figured that was about all the room we could spare."

Noble didn't let on, but he'd clean forgotten Christmas was only a week away. With everything that had happened in the last year, and especially the last three months, he'd been focused on nothing but figuring a way to keep him and Matt out of the poorhouse.

Thank you, Lord. At least we accomplished that.

THE NEXT MORNING, he made up a quick excuse about needing a few things from town and had expected to ride in alone, but both Matt and Gracie mentioned they could use another trip. While this would make shopping for surprise Christmas presents next to impossible, he figured he'd better try.

He started at the feed store, hoping to send Gracie and Matt off on their own errands. "I'll get the horse feed and other things. You two go on and knock around for an hour or so. I'll meet you at the mercantile." That would give him an excuse for being there and, Lord willing, he could buy and hide their presents before they showed up.

To pass a minute or two until his party had wandered out of sight, he ambled over to the livestock corral, curious what was coming up for sale. He was eyeing a swirling mass of antsy Longhorns when Miss Jillian Weatherspoon flounced up beside him in a flurry of pink lace and ribbons. The woman didn't appear to have a problem with overdressing, and he wondered that she didn't have on a coat.

"Good morning, Mr. McCain. I saw you from the window. Come to buy some feed for those horses?"

"Yes, ma'am, just two bags." He took his gaze back to the corral and surveyed a heifer and her little bull with half-interest. "After Christmas I think we'll be back to get a few head of cattle and maybe a hog."

"We'll be here." She looked up at Noble with shimmering blue eyes, long lashes a-fluttering.

Her open flirting was surprising. The little gal had to be a handful for her parents.

"I heard you and Gracie got married by the judge not the minister. Any particular reason?"

Noble raised his brow at her boldness. "Some folks would say that's not any of your business.

"Some folks say a lot of things aren't my business, but I see what's going on in this town. All these widows marrying out of need or convenience. I don't think any of them are in love."

"Well, whether they stood before a man of God or a man of the law, they made vows. You don't break vows. At least I don't." He held her gaze just until he saw understanding dawn, then he touched his hat. "I'll grab those bags of feed now." He started toward the store but when he looked up, he realized Gracie and Matt were standing on the porch, watching, both of them stone-faced, but Noble detected their disapproval.

"Matt asked if I would take him for an ice cream. I wanted to make sure that was all right with you." Gracie's gaze slid slowly to the girl beside Noble. "Good afternoon, Gwendolyn."

Jillian's icy expression changed to red hot anger and she made a sudden move toward Gracie. Noble shot his hand out, stopping her. "That'll be fine, Gracie. Just one scoop, though, son. Don't ruin your appetite."

"I'm not five, Pa," the boy snapped back and glanced coolly at Miss Weatherspoon. A boy trying to impress a pretty face. Understandable but not excusable.

Noble straightened up and shot Matt a scowl. "You're not man enough to talk to me like that."

Gracie nudged the boy and whispered out of the side of her mouth, "Apologize."

Matt huffed but obliged, deflating a little. "Sorry. Didn't meant to sass you, Pa."

"It's all right. Now go on, and be at the mercantile in an hour."

"Yes, sir." He and Gracie turned and trudged down the boardwalk.

"Well, he might not have your manners, but your son certainly has your looks."

Noble gave a moment's thought to telling Miss Weatherspoon to go and sit in a trough of cold water but decided instead to ignore her behavior. After all, it was nothing to him. He touched the brim of his hat once more in goodbye. "Ma'am." Without a glance back, he left her standing there alone.

10

Gracie tried to focus on Matt's company and the sweet ice cream—which was good even on a cold day—but her attention drifted over and over to Noble and that little witch Jillian. She sighed. She probably shouldn't call the girl such an unfriendly name.

"Your ice cream not any good?" Matt asked from across the café table, his spoon full of vanilla ice cream.

"No, it's wonderful." She finished off the last of her chocolate and licked the spoon. "I'm glad we did this."

"Yeah, me, too. I don't get sweets too often…anymore."

"Did your mother bake a lot?"

"Yes, ma'am. Made the best cherry pie you've ever had."

"I'm sure she did. Maybe I'll work on my own baking skills."

"You could." He flashed her a toothy grin, stark white against his dark skin. It hinted at the handsome young man that would be born of this gawky teenager. "But you can do things she couldn't. You've got gifts, too."

The comment took Gracie back. She'd never thought of her skills as a gift. Betsy crossed her mind. A sick little girl who was given a few minutes of sheer delight. Maybe that was a gift…

"If you don't mind, Miss Gracie, I'd kinda like to wander around town on my own for a few minutes."

"No, not at all. I might do the same thing." Especially since the seed of an idea had just sprouted in her mind.

Gracie strode down Grand Platte Road, turned at the sheriff's office, and walked up to the intersection with Center Ave. Right where the two streets met, a dark, empty, brick building stared out at the town. Old, yellowing newspapers covered the windows. She tried the door without any hope, and it was indeed locked. With a sigh, she stepped back and looked up at the second floor. Vacant, soulless windows reflected the gray sky above her.

It was in a fine location, sitting between the sheriff's office on one end of Stagecoach Road and the sheriff's house at the other end. The butcher shop was just across the alley, and the livery was one building over from there. Everyone in town eventually needed the sheriff, the butcher, or the livery. They would all pass through this area.

Daydreaming now, Gracie stepped to the edge of the boardwalk and imagined a marquis painted on the front of the building: Last Chance Community Theater in bold, red letters. Beneath that in large type, *Romeo and Juliet*.

No. She shook her head. Waving her hand at the imaginary sign, the title *The Comedy of Errors* appeared. *Last Chance could use the humor.*

"Something I can help you with, miss?"

Gracie blushed and dropped her hand. "No. I'm... daydreaming, to be honest."

"Oh. You interested in the building?"

"What? No. No—but, it's for sale?"

The man, tall, thin, in his thirties but sporting streaks of gray in his mustache, offered his hand. "I'm Harold Purcell. I own this building."

"Gracie Erst—I mean, Gracie McCain. And I was just window-shopping, you could say."

"Oh." He fished a key ring from his vest pocket. "I've got five minutes before my next appointment, if you'd like to look inside."

She had five minutes, too, but what was the point? While the location of this building was perfect, it probably would need too much work to make it into a true theater. "It's a lovely building and the location is grand, but I doubt it fits my plan."

"And what is that, if I may ask?"

"Well, someday, I'd like to open a theater. Teach acting and perform plays, and eventually bring in professional troupes for entertainment."

"And what kind of floor plan would you'd say you need for that?"

Memories of a dozen grand opera halls and theaters stampeded free across Gracie's mind, but this building was a third the size of those venues. Then again, Last Chance wasn't Denver or San Francisco...

"Oh, a high ceiling to allow for rigging lights and curtains, walls to create a backstage area, and lobby. Enough seating for a hundred people. That would do for Last Chance, I think."

"Mrs. McCain, I think you should allow yourself a look."

He held the key up in front of her. It glimmered magically, hypnotically.

What was the harm in just looking? "All right."

To Gracie's amazement, Mr. Purcell's building was one large, open unfinished space. A blank slate. But was it big enough to be even a small theater?

"Picture this," Mr. Purcell said, walking to the center of the room, which was a good hundred feet long and wide. Two large support beams stood on each side, twenty or so feet from the walls. Not ideal in a theater, but not a disaster. And, intriguing her, two large barn doors were set in the back wall. Ideal for moving in large sets…someday.

His back to Gracie, Mr. Purcell waved his hands at the back wall like a magician performing a magic trick. "An elevated stage here. A backstage area there. House lights ringing the stage." He turned to her. "Two rows of pews." He started walking toward her, counting out loud, and stopped at twenty. "Two rows, twenty pews each. And just behind you," he pointed, and she turned. "A lobby. Small, but accommodating enough, I would think."

"I suppose…" she said hesitantly.

"And there is a full floor over our heads. Plenty of storage."

Oh, yes, Gracie had to admit it. The building could be tweaked enough to provide Last Chance with a fine little theater. She could see it, too, as if it were real. Velvet curtains, glimmering wallpaper, flickering lights, a crowd of townsfolk murmuring as they settled into the seats, excitement in the air.

"What would you say to twenty dollars a month?"

That it might as well be a hundred dollars a month. "I told you, Mr. Purcell, I'm just window-shopping. But someday…" She let her gaze drift dreamily over the room. "This building would do fine." A little construction to bring it around, but not much. "What was it supposed to be?"

"I had and may still have plans for a furniture store. The death of so many men has slowed our economy, as you might guess. The widows are choosing husbands, not sofas and coffee tables. Eventually, Last Chance will need a furniture store but not yet."

"Yes." She sighed. "Not yet." She glanced around the room again and whispered softly, "The venom clamours of a jealous woman Poisons more deadly than a mad dog's tooth."

"Pardon me, what's that?"

"Oh, nothing. Just a line from *The Comedy of Errors*." She shook herself out of the memory and smiled at the man. "I played a part once."

"Oh, I see," he said, chuckling. "Double, double toil and something-or-other. I saw Macbe—"

"Stop," Gracie thrust out her hand.

Mr. Purcell stepped back, eyes as round as a scared mule's. "I'm sorry?"

"No, I'm sorry. I didn't mean to overreact. It's just that it's a superstition in the theater. Never say the name of that particular play or quote a line from it. It will bring a curse."

"Oh, my apologies."

"It's all right. Just a superstition." She offered her hand, and they shook their goodbye. "Thank you for showing me this building. I'll keep it mind."

"I hope you get your theater, Mrs. McCain."

"And I hope you get your furniture store, Mr. Purcell."

AFTER THE ICE cream with Miss Gracie, Matt excused himself to wander around Last Chance, maybe take another gander at that saddle. He was coming down the walk when the three men in front of him stepped off into the street. They opened up a path that led to Miss Weatherspoon talking in a pretty fussy tone with a man wearing a badge on his chest. Matt ducked beside a display of brooms.

"What do we know about her really, Sheriff? She and her husband were obviously some kind of vagabonds. Probably even hucksters. And I'm telling you, she took my bracelet the other day at church. At church. I mean slid it right off my wrist like a professional pickpocket."

"Now, Miss Jillian, that's a strong accusation. You also said she gave it back to you. Now, don't you think it's possible it actually did fall off your wrist?"

"It never has before."

"Jewelry falls off ladies all the time. Folks turn it in at the office. Not unusual at all."

Miss Weatherspoon crossed her arms tightly across her chest and tapped her foot. Matt thought she looked madder than a bee trapped in a jar. "She performed an interesting little trick yesterday for Bet—"

"I saw. I was there. She gave a dying child some wonderful moments of laughter." He leaned a little closer to the woman. "That isn't helping your case."

"You think just because she entertained a sick child, she's some kind of saint?"

"Doesn't make her look much like a thief."

Miss Weatherspoon growled at the man. "She's not who she says she is—or not *what* she says she is. I'll prove it."

"I don't know that she's said much of anything at all, the way she keeps to herself. In fact, her spending time with Betsy was the most outgoing and friendly thing I've seen the woman do since she got here."

"Exactly. She's gone out of her way to avoid people."

"Can't imagine what would make her want to do that."

Matt smirked at the the sheriff's sarcasm.

"You are not doing your job, Sheriff."

"My job hasn't kicked in yet, leastwise not with Mrs. Erst

—I mean, what is it? Mrs. McCain? If she steps out of line, if she so much as jay walks, I'll treat her the same as any other law breaker."

"That's not good enough, Sheriff. Not at all." But before the sheriff could argue, the girl was stomping down the boardwalk like some kind of crazy, pink bull. Matt wanted to laugh at the image but knew this wasn't a laughing matter. Jillian Weatherspoon had it in for Miss Gracie.

Was it over Pa? he wondered. She'd have better luck *riding* a pink bull for all the attention she'd get from him. He'd given his word to Miss Gracie, and in a McCain's world, his word was iron.

11

Christmas morning was a quiet affair, and a little awkward for Gracie. She'd never celebrated it the way Noble and Matt did. She sat quietly as Noble read what he called The Christmas Story from the Bible. She looked out the little window at the snow gently falling, and enjoyed the soothing, deep sound of his voice as he read about a baby born in a manger.

The Savior of mankind starting out life in such lowly circumstances. This fascinated Gracie, because while she didn't know much about Jesus, she knew He ended His life hanging on a cross. What happened in between?

Curious now, she planned to listen more closely to the

little Bible lessons father and son did every night. She might even pick up the Bible herself sometime today.

First, they enjoyed a breakfast of eggs, pancakes, cinnamon rolls, bacon and coffee. The cinnamon rolls were Gracie's special addition to the menu in honor of the day. Then they all opened their presents. The boys went first and seemed truly appreciative of their socks and gloves. Noble flicked out the blade on his new, significantly larger pocketknife, and grinned with pleasure.

Holding it up to the light, he admired the blade. "A real pocketknife." He winked at her. "Thank you."

"If you're going to carry a knife, it should be good for more than cleaning your nails."

He chuckled and watched as Matt pulled his gift free of the butcher paper wrapping. "Oh, a Bowie knife." The long blade glinted in the light. "Thank you. That'll be handy. My skinning knife is about worn out."

"Next year, I'm sure I'll have a better idea of what you two need."

"These are fine gifts," Noble assured her. He slapped Matt on the shoulder. "And I know you were eyeing a saddle, son, but maybe for your birthday in the fall."

"Sure, Pa. I understand."

But a hesitation in his voice made Gracie wonder if he did. She saw Noble flinch, indicating he was a little hurt. Moving past the moment, though, he pulled a large, flat package from behind his back. "For you, Miss Gracie. From the both of us."

"Oh, thank you." She tore off the wrapping and was moved by the sight of the book. "Shakespeare's Plays, Volume One."

"We're hoping you'll read from it sometime. Better entertainment than knitting."

She laughed. Matt joined in and she noticed Noble watching them with a half-smile playing on his lips. The real, sincere laughter of friends sharing secret jokes. Maybe this was going to work after all. They might not be a family, but they were becoming friends. Gracie hoped that meant Noble's trust in her was growing.

"Well, I hate to interrupt this party," he slapped his thighs and stood, "but I want to throw the stock some extra feed."

"I'll help you, Pa." Matt moved to set his knife aside, but Noble waved him off.

"Nah. It's Christmas. You stay here and take a day off. It's a gift."

NOBLE SUITED UP in his coat and gloves and headed out. The day was bitter, but his heart was light and it made the pain of tending the stock a lot easier. Gracie had some bad habits, but his confidence she could shed them was growing.

"And I know she's listening, Lord," he said, throwing hay into the center of the corral. The horses nickered and whinnied with approval and ate greedily. "When we pick up the Bible, she's not turning such a deaf ear anymore." He used the handle of the pitchfork to bust the ice in the trough. Cold as it was, he'd have to do it again by nightfall. He tended to the hog, tossing her some grain and a few leftovers, then headed back to the wagon.

He stomped the snow off at the door and let himself in… and froze. Gracie and Matt were sitting at the little table, and she was shuffling a deck of cards like…like a professional. She fanned out the cards, made them stand up in a wave, then swept them into her hand and sent them sailing, almost as if by magic, from one hand to the other, in a long, flowing train. She didn't look up until she'd completed the shuffle.

And Noble knew the look on his face was what froze her hands in place. Matt gulped. Noble slowly approached them. "What are you two doing?"

She hesitated before answering. He watched as she shoved

the fear and concern out of her expression and came back with an obstinate raise of her chin. "I'm teaching him a skill. A handy skill."

"You're teaching my son to gamble." Noble could barely contain his anger.

"I asked her, Pa." Matt shot to his feet. "Don't get angry at her. What if I don't want to be a farmer all my life? What if I want to be a cowboy? Cowboys play poker and I don't want to lose my shirt."

The glare Noble set on Matt had the boy backing up. Then he shifted his heated gaze to Gracie. "My son is not going to hang about in saloons."

Gracie rose to her feet slowly and began shuffling the cards again with alacrity and skill that was almost astonishing. "I don't know where your son will hang about, but he may not always be under your thumb, Noble. I can teach him how not to get rolled in a friendly game. No tricks. No cheating. Knowing how to play poker is an honest skill."

"One that you will not be teaching my son. Do you understand?"

She stopped the cards abruptly. "Perfectly." Then, surprising Noble, the steam went out of her. She exhaled softly and tapped the deck against the palm of her hand. "I'm sorry. I should have asked you. He's your son."

"And I've got a mind of my own. I'm going to chop some wood." Matt cut between them, leveling a glare on Noble as he stomped outside.

Gracie felt terrible. She hated to be the cause of such turmoil, but the boundaries around here were unnatural to her. She didn't know how to read the signs. "I'm sorry. That's my fault. I crossed a line again."

Noble looked around the wagon as if he was desperate for a place to flee. But there was no privacy here. Finally, he hung his head and Gracie waited for another berating.

He surprised her by giving her, instead, a calm, reasoned response. "Just...ask me next time. Please."

December 25, 1878

Dear Stacy,

I hope this letter finds you healthy and prosperous. I know it's been sometime since we've talked, but I am toying with the idea of opening a theater and, of course, thought of you. It is not in the near future, but I am formulating plans.

First, let me catch you up. Melvin and I moved to Last Chance, Nebraska. We retired from the business and were going to farm. Or, should I say, at least <u>he</u> retired. I still desire to act and had hoped our farm might be a way to finance a second business.

Melvin, however, was killed in September in a blizzard. As were many of the men in this town. I found myself in an odd situation. To keep the land we were going to file on for our homestead, I had to marry a perfect stranger.

I suppose I've done worse things. Or at least more foolish things.

Mr. Noble McCain and I, however, have more of a mutually agreed upon business arrangement than a marriage. He is a knowledgeable farmer who fell on hard times. Perhaps you see now, we have helped each other out. I had the land and a little money. He had the skills and the strong back. Oh, and he has a son.

He's an interesting man. Straight and true. A moral code that is set in stone. That's been the hardest thing to get used to and I've made a few missteps with him. I taught his son a simple magic trick. When that went well, I thought I'd teach the boy a little about poker. A good card player never starves.

I saw the lesson as a service to my fellow man. Noble (how apt the name) accused me of corrupting the boy.

I'm confident we'll get past these miscommunications, as long as I can unlearn some bad habits. But I digress.

Mr. McCain is also determined and will make the land pay. I'm sure of it, and eventually I'll have the funds to start up my own theater. I even looked at a building today that would serve well for a small venue.

My purpose in writing you is to ascertain your whereabouts and determine if you are still acting. I hope Grandma Goodman is well and able to forward this letter to you, wherever you may be keeping yourself currently. Out of trouble, I hope. Speaking for myself, those days are behind me now.

I'm eager to hear from you. Write soon. Merry Christmas.

Love,

Gracie

12

———

The end of January disappeared in a constant flurry of snow-storms, but at least the temperature didn't turn horribly cold. Still, getting the logs cut and stacked to transform the run-in shed to a barn was grueling work. Gracie, Noble was quick to appreciate, at least made sure her men had hot food to warm them up every night.

The weather took a vicious turn for the worst on February fourteenth. So cold and windy, Noble and Matt couldn't do anything but tend to the animals in the unfinished barn. They tucked the horses together in the back stall for warmth, tossed them and the hog some feed, busted the ice in the troughs just before dark, and hurried back to the wagon.

They found a stew simmering on the stove and Gracie mixing up dough for cookies, but her movements were jerky, and tense. Noble noted a pinch in her forehead. The wagon was cool, struggling against the weather outside to maintain its warmth. He and Matt hung their coats at the door then Matt slipped by Gracie to claim a spot on the bench near the stove.

"I think I'll read for a spell," he said, picking up his dime novel from the table. "Unless you need something, Pa?"

"No." He moved to slide behind Gracie. "Excuse me."

"Certainly."

He started to put his hands on her hips as she pressed closer to the stove but caught himself. This dance was getting a little more maddening with each new performance. Every time they slipped by each other, he found it harder and harder to keep his hands to himself. Ignoring the thoughts that bounced around in his brain when he brushed up against her was becoming a losing battle.

He was getting distracted by the gentle curve of her waist, her pale, smooth throat, silky, blonde hair—he winced. Noticing such things was only going to make it harder to see her as the boss. Or just a business partner. Whatever she wanted to call herself, she was also a beautiful woman.

Holding back a sigh, he joined Matt at the table and pulled his notebook from the shelf above the window. This was what he called his Grand Plan. He wrote ideas and tasks in here to keep him focused—

A harsh gust of wind hit the wagon, making it shudder, and Gracie gasped. Noble saw her tense up and he realized the storm had her worried. She was afraid of another blizzard.

Noble reached across the table and tapped Matt's hand. When he pulled his attention from the dime novel, Noble gestured with his head at Gracie.

Matt frowned, not understanding.

"Gracie," Noble said, "I don't suppose there's any chance we could talk you into performing something for us? Get our minds off the storm?"

She glanced over her shoulder at them. "Oh, I'd love to. Let me get these in the oven." She was spooning the cookies on to a tray.

Again, Noble gestured at Matt, who finally got it. "Oh. Oh, yeah, I can do that, Miss Gracie."

"What? Are you sure?"

"If I can lick the bowl."

"All right." They did the side-step to get by each other and she pulled her Christmas present of Shakespeare plays from her bed. "Let's see…" What hadn't she done for them that might not bore a teenage boy? An idea struck her, and she put the book down. Noble tilted his head. She smiled at him and picked up Matt's Dime novel.

"Black Bart and the Bandits of the Box B Ranch, or Sheriff Randall's Revenge."

Matt's head swiveled around. "You going to perform that?"

She flipped through the story, chuckled at some of the language, but nodded. "I've never done one of these before. I'll give it a try."

Noble watched her as she quickly read the first few pages. He liked the way she always bit her bottom lip when she was thinking hard. And then, he noted, she twisted strands of gold around her finger when a decision was imminent. He tried not to let his eyes drift over her pleasing curves, her tiny waist.

He blinked and cleared his head. "Will this performance be tonight?"

She narrowed her eyes at him. "Have some place to go?"

The wind howled as if to mock him. "I guess not."

Matt shoved the cookies into the oven. "I'm ready."

Gracie opened the book and began to read. "Chapter One.

A most vile and notorious character is a cattle thief. Black Bart was reputed to be the most vile, fearless, and clever of them all. He hated all men and took whatever cattle he chose…"

Noble scooted over so Matt could join him on this side of the table. Both of them listened with rapt attention, smiling here and there at Gracie's dramatic presentation.

"'No, no, sir, I beg you." She pressed the back of her hand to her forehead and looked away from the story. "Please don't take my cattle. They're all I have in the world to feed my young son."

She came back to the story and turned her voice gravelly for the character. "Black Bart leered at the beautiful rancher. 'They're my cattle now, gal.'

'Stop, you worthless creature,' cried Sheriff Randall. 'You won't take one head of cattle from this kind lady.'"

Gracie read until they smelled the cookies. Matt saved them at the last minute and pulled them from the oven. A little browner than they should have been, but not burnt. In the pause, Gracie rubbed her arms.

"Yeah, it's getting a little chillier. Matt, toss a log on the fire." Matt set the cookies on top of the stove and did as instructed.

"Shall I stop?" Gracie asked.

Noble and Matt shook their heads. "You read good," Matt told her, "It's almost like a play."

"Agreed. You're very entertaining." Noble tamped down his enthusiasm because he was, in truth, entranced by her little show. So much so, he was almost bewildered by the pleasure he derived from watching her.

"My feet are getting cold," Matt muttered, wiggling his toes in his wool socks.

"I have an idea." Gracie eyed her bed. "Matt, bring the cookies."

Noble's mouth fell open. Was she suggesting they…? He waited to see.

She let down the bed, barely giving Noble a second to pull his notebook off the table. She climbed up and grinned at them. "I don't bite. We'll sit up here. Heat rises. It's warm."

Matt lifted his feet in quick succession. "You don't have to tell me twice." He grabbed the tray of cookies and brought it with him. Settling at the foot of the bed, he placed the tray in the center. Gracie sat cross-legged, against her pillow, the dime novel in her lap.

Something about this idea greatly appealed to Noble…and scared him at the same time.

Gracie patted the mattress beside her. "That long frame of yours will have to bend a little, but you'll fit."

"It's worth it, Pa," Matt said, peeling up a warm cookie. "It's nicer, for sure."

Acting like he wasn't sure he was going to enjoy this, he put his notebook back on the shelf and climbed up slowly into the tight space. "I don't know about this."

Gracie smacked the pillow beside her. "Where's your sense of adventure? I have an audience and I'm not letting you go. *It*," she corrected quickly. "I'm not letting it go."

She dropped her eyes to the novel. Noble felt the twitch of a wry grin and fought it back. He settled on his side, resting his head on his knuckles. "You're right. This is cozy."

He wondered if it was his imagination that their gazes lingered. Gracie cleared her throat and started reading again. Little by little, though Noble was enjoying the story, the warmth, the company, and the hypnotic cadence of her voice, sleep tugged at him.

When he drifted off to sleep from Gracie's show exactly, he had no idea. For a while he dreamed. Dreamed of Black Bart trying to steal cattle from Jessie. Noble rode to the rescue. She kissed him, grateful for his heroic effort. She felt so good in his arms, yet thin, like a fading memory, almost like smoke, a dream tinged with sadness. Then, in the odd way of dreams, the woman in his arms changed suddenly from Jessie to Gracie. And she felt as real as his own breath. His hands traced her cheeks, her shoulders, slipped around her waist and snugged her close. She turned in his arms, leaned her body back against him, and pulled his left arm around her.

"Yes," she whispered so softly he almost didn't hear her. "I'm warm now."

NOBLE BLINKED. He was looking at the back of Gracie's head, her golden braid glittering in the morning light. He became aware of the length of her pressed against him. His left arm was draped over her. His right arm was folded under the pillow, holding it in place.

She breathed, shifted slightly…and he realized this was no dream. He froze as if he were curled up with a bear and didn't dare wake it.

I must have fallen asleep…

He allowed himself a moment to appreciate the warmth of her, the comfortable way she fit against him. Curves, and softness. She smelled like sugar cookies. A gust of wind moaned past the wagon, haunting and forlorn, as if to mock his predicament.

He was in a terrible spot…one desperately difficult to crawl away from. She was like a radiator and lying here with her was a thousand times better than going outside to the biting cold and slicing wind.

But he couldn't stay here. What if she woke up? How could he explain this?

Movement at his feet baffled him for a moment, until he realized Matt was asleep crosswise on the end of the mattress. Noble raised his head. Gracie still held on to the dime novel with one hand. The other hand…

He realized she had his left hand pressed against her chest. Their fingers were tangled.

Oh, boy…

He could lie here all day. Desperately he wished he could surrender to the situation and stay with her in his arms. If he could keep it a secret, he would. If she woke now…this would be too awkward to explain.

Lamenting what he had to do, bewildered how he and Gracie had so naturally taken up this position, he moved. Slowly. As if his life depended on her staying asleep. He freed a finger. Then another.

Eventually, still moving at glacial speed, he slipped from under the covers into the cold light of dawn. And a cold wagon. As quietly as he could, he stoked the fire, pleased to see there were still embers in the stove. The fire would start and warm the wagon quickly.

But the heat it let off was nothing compared to what he'd felt under the covers with Gracie. He rubbed his neck and shook his head. *I am in trouble, Lord. Give me the strength to keep this…*

He glanced over at her. The feminine shape evident beneath the quilt. The dip of her waist. The slope up to her hip. What did he want Gracie to be? A boss? A friend?

Something more? Had this feeling been here the whole time? Was that why he'd so easily agreed to a marriage of convenience?

Lord, I guess the best prayer is, help me figure this out so no one gets hurt. Especially Matt.

"I'm sorry," Faith Thornton, the postmistress, said, her pretty, delicate face blushing with unspoken questions. "Nothing for you again."

Gracie felt foolish for all the recent stops she'd made at the post office. After the third time checking for a letter from Stacy, she could tell the woman was bubbling over with curiosity. And since she ran the post office and telegraph office from her home, not chatting for a moment did seem rude even to Gracie.

She sagged a little and Faith seemed to take it as an opening to probe the matter. "I don't mean to pry, but if I knew what I was looking for—a package versus a letter, for example—I'd know if I should run it out to you."

"You'd do that?"

"Certainly. This seems important to you."

"That's very kind of you."

Faith smiled, a warm, genuine expression. "I heard what you did for Betsy. That was kind. If I could deliver a package to you, what a small way to say thank you."

"Oh, well, um, it's just a letter. From someone…I used to know. But I haven't seen her in so long, I don't know if she even got my letter."

Faith patted her hand. "I'll keep a look out. And you should do more of your little shows for the children. So many of them have lost parents…a puppet show or really any entertainment would bring them such joy."

Betsy's innocent, giddy laughter echoed in Gracie's ears. Even now it made her smile. "Thank you, Faith. I'll think about your suggestion."

Gracie pulled her coat a little tighter and stepped out into the snowy day. Gentle flurries swirled about and the temperature hovered in the low thirties. All in all, not bad for late February in Nebraska.

Planning the rest of her errands, she strode up the street toward the mercantile when hooting and hollering broke out as she crossed an alley. She tracked the sound and caught sight of a group of boys, wild as a band of Indians, racing across the opening. Running, leaping, whooping, and hollering. With mixed emotions over their rowdy behavior, she still gave them a little smile. *You're only young once—*

She gasped as the last boy with the group raced by. The smile melted away and her mouth fell open. Though the snow did obscure her view some, she was certain she recognized the last hooligan.

Now, what was Matt doing with a disorderly bunch like that?

Gracie bit her lip, considered following the boys, but backed off the idea. She wasn't his mother and he wasn't really doing anything wrong. Still, if Noble found out, there would be words.

She vacillated for a moment, but decided in the end to let Matt go about his business. If she had the chance, she would ask about his new friends and say something motherly like *the right friends can determine your destiny.*

Oh, how true were those words and she hoped the boy would heed them.

"MATT MCCAIN, I'll have words with you, son."

Matt looked up from his chore of chopping wood, stopping the ax in mid-swing. "Yes, Pa?"

"The sheriff stopped me in town today. Said he saw you running with a crew of boys that are known for causing trouble." Behind him, the door to the wagon opened and he sensed Gracie watching. "I expect you to choose better friends."

"Ah, you don't even know them." Matt swung and lodged the ax in the block. "All you ever want me to do is hang around with those mealy-mouthed kids from church. You don't ever want me to have any fun."

"That's not true. But I want you to choose your friends wise—"

"We're not all perfect, Pa. But these boys aren't what Sheriff—"

"If the sheriff says they're trouble, they're trouble—"

"Boys, boys." Grace rushed over, drying her hands on a dish rag. "Do I have to get the Chinese finger trap out again?"

"He's breathing down my neck, Miss Gracie. He won't let me do anything, go anywhere—"

"He's your father and he is giving you good advice." She

lifted those pretty green eyes up to Noble. "And he's just trying to find his way. You could give him a little space."

"I gave him some space and he's running with riff-raff."

"You don't know them well enough to say that, Pa. I haven't seen them do anything bad. Other than get a little loud."

"The sheriff said—"

"Those boys talk big, but they haven't done anything in front of me. The sheriff doesn't know diddly squat and neither do you."

"Matt," Gracie snapped.

"Son, I'll—"

Gracie rested her hand on Noble's arm to quiet him as she tried to do the same for Matt. "Your father only has your best interest at heart. You have no idea how important it is to choose the right friends. They can set the direction of your life if you let them." She gave Matt a look. "Now, apologize."

Matt shook his head, but it melted into a slight nod. "Sorry, Pa."

Noble almost backed up at the quick surrender, which was much better than repeating the Chinese finger trap. But he held still, flicked a perplexed glance at Gracie, and then nodded, too. "I forgive you. I'm sorry for judging your friends."

"Sure." Matt picked up the ax and went back to his chore.

Noble didn't know what look was on his face, but he cut his eyes at Gracie, a little bewildered by her gentle, peace-making skills and simple words of wisdom. Even with her slightly mixed-up moral compass, Gracie was having a positive impact on Matt.

He walked by her, leading his horse, and muttered, "Thank you."

14

———

Noble sat down on the top of the butte and stared out at the rolling horizon, washed in the rays of the setting sun. For the first time in months, the air was friendly, warm. Green grass and wildflowers sprouted tenaciously from the dirt beside him.

That same dirt filled his fingernails, streaked his face, and highlighted the wrinkles in his clothing. His back ached from plowing. His arm hurt from the hammering they'd done first thing this morning. He glanced over his shoulder. At least the barn was nearly finished. It lacked a few pieces of siding on the back but Matt and Gracie could handle that.

Spring was breaking, and they had to be ready to plant.

He sighed heavily at the thought. Between building the barn for the livestock, buying the livestock, and feeding all these hungry mouths, and making the initial purchase of seed, Gracie's money had not gone as far as Noble had hoped.

"My, that's a grim expression."

He started at Gracie's voice, but didn't look at her.

"Here, I thought you could use a cup of coffee." She handed him the steaming mug and then, to his surprise, sat down beside him. "You look troubled."

"We're almost out of money."

"I know."

"I was doing some calculating today while I was plowing. I haven't bought enough seed for the yields I want."

"And that means…?"

"Our first harvest is going to be slim. Real slim."

She wrapped her dress around her ankles and drew her knees up. "You're saying there won't be anything extra? As in, for my theater?"

"There won't be extra for much of anything."

She accepted this news quietly, which made Noble feel even worse. He'd hoped to give her something to tuck away, but he didn't see it happening. The yields he was projecting— they might be able to stand one hailstorm, but if the summer was violent, they weren't going to have any extra."

"You warned me it might take some time."

"You're not disappointed?"

"Disappointed? Certainly, a little. I'm more surprised you're so downhearted. You warned me this would be a long, difficult row to hoe, making a farm profitable."

"Just a little more would have gotten us over the hump. If I had anything to sell, I would, but we need all the tools I brought with us."

Gracie laid a hand on his shoulder and smiled. "We'll figure it out."

He was taken for a second by the warmth of her hand, and

by the sunset light playing in her shimmering hair. Her eyes, up close, were as green as the first buds of Kansas wheat. And he smelled cinnamon on her breath.

He took a sip of the coffee to redirect his thoughts. "We'll figure it out. I'm going to have that put on my tombstone."

Gracie laughed and climbed to her feet. "Here lies Noble McCain," she recited. "He figured it out. A little too late."

"Thanks a lot." He chucked a clod of dirt at her feet and she squealed.

"Any time," she tossed over her shoulder at him as she scrambled down the hill back to the wagon.

GRACIE SHOVELED the eggs from the frying pan onto the plate in front of Noble and returned the pan to the stove. "Noble, I've got an idea." She cracked two more eggs and they sizzled violently in the bacon grease. She used the sound to buy a moment before she spoke her mind. She wasn't sure how her *husband* would react. She knew what Melvin would say, but he didn't figure into this anymore.

Noble cocked his head to one side and smirked at Gracie. "You going to tell me or make me guess?"

Matt chuckled at the friendly banter and took a bite of his eggs. "She's dragging it out. Must be good."

Gracie turned and waved her spatula at them. "What if I did a show? Something to entertain the children. We could put the money I raise toward more seed."

Noble stopped with a fork midway to his mouth. Gracie held her breath. She could hear Melvin: *That's not where I want to put my focus.*

"You think you could make any money doing that?"

"Sure, she could, Pa," Matt said with enthusiasm. "A few magic tricks—"

"Tell a story with puppets," Gracie said. "Maybe even do a scene from a play."

"Puppets," Matt said. "You'd have every kid in town there. Except for us older ones, of course."

"Of course."

"Kids don't have any money," Noble said, tearing his biscuit in half.

Gracie flipped her eggs, pondering the problem. "No, but their parents do. And Faith Thornton suggested the idea. A lot of people would probably like to see the children entertained for a bit. They've been through so much."

He shrugged. "Probably true. You should look into it."

Gracie had to hold back a giddy shout of joy. Not that she needed Noble's permission necessarily, but she had it. And it made a difference to her enthusiasm. She could count on one hand how many people had ever supported her acting dreams, and two of them were sitting at the table.

"I'll help, Miss Gracie," Matt offered.

"Long as it doesn't take you from the farm chores…too much," Noble said.

Lost in thought now, her mind whirling with potential ideas and presentations, Gracie took her eggs and sat down. "I could use his help," she said absently. "It won't interfere." She looked up at Matt. "We could work on it in the evenings."

"It?"

"Whatever it might be."

GRACIE TOOK a breath and tried to calm her racing heart. Her palms were slick with sweat. Beside her in the pew, Noble and Matt looked cool as cucumbers. Why not? They didn't have to stand up in front of half the town and pitch an idea to which strangers might react just like Melvin always did.

On the other hand, maybe they'd react the way Noble and Matt had. They had given Gracie a glimpse of what was possible, what it felt like when someone gave your dream a chance. It was intoxicating. Only one other person in her whole life had ever understood—

"Well, unless there is any new business," Pastor Collins scanned the crowded sanctuary. "We'll close the meeting with prayer to God our Heavenly Father…"

Noble nudged Gracie. It took her a second to understand the poke, and then she realized Pastor Collins seemed to be waiting on something. Her cue. She raised her gloved hand slowly.

The motion caught his eye and he nodded at Gracie. "Mrs. Erst—I mean, Mrs. McCain, you have some new business?"

She exhaled her nervousness and rose to address the hundred or so people at the meeting. "Yes, thank you." She licked her lips. "My name is Gracie McCain. Most of you probably don't know me, but have probably seen me around. Um, I have a background in…the theater. I would like to do a show to entertain the children. Give them something to smile about. I have some puppets, even a small stage, and maybe I could do some magic tricks. I was wondering what the town would think of that."

"I think it's a wonderful idea," Faith Thornton said from somewhere in the back, though Gracie couldn't find her in the crowd.

"I saw how you entertained Betsy," a man's voice rose up and Gracie tracked it to the sheriff, a couple of pews back. "Haven't seen her light up like that in months."

"It's true," a woman said. Gracie turned toward the front. Betsy's mother, Ruth. "Betsy is still talking about your mustache trick, Mrs. McCain. Thank you. She'll be tickled senseless to hear you want to do something else."

"Mrs. McCain?" A hand shot up, attached to Millie Taylor, rising to address her question to Gracie. "Would it be possible for you to put a little something in your show for us adults? We don't get out much." The room rumbled with laughter.

"What I mean is, I bet us ladies would love a chance to dress up a little, maybe have dinner with our families at Dawson's Diner. You know, make an evening of it."

Nods and a round of approving applause swept the room. Millie grinned at Gracie, raised her eyebrows in a hopeful *please-say-yes* kind of way, and then sat back down.

Gracie's mind raced. "Um, well, yes, I'm sure I could do something for an older audience as well. A little Shakespeare maybe, but I should mention…I'd like to charge for the show. We're trying to get our farm established and could use the money."

"How much?" a man asked, sounding skeptical.

"I was thinking two cents a person or five cents for a family?" Was it too much? She'd given it a lot of thought. It should be five cents a person, but Last Chance had to warm to the idea of live entertainment—

"Oh, all right. That's not so bad," the man said. A mumble of agreement circulated through the audience.

"When do you think you'll do this production," Heather Barnes asked without standing, since she was only one pew back.

"I'm not exactly sure." She glanced at Noble. He needed to buy seed. Soon. But she could only do so much and make the plan worthwhile. "I more or less wanted to gauge interest tonight."

"Well, we're interested," a man shouted from the back. "We need some entertainment after the winter we've just had."

Again, voices rose in agreement, but louder this time, and the applause was more enthusiastic. Her heart soaring, Gracie glanced at Noble. He was grinning and clapping too. He was happy for her and it nearly took her breath away. If not for the crowd, she would have hugged him…maybe even kissed that grinning mouth.

The applause intruded on her train of thought and she

snapped back to the moment. "As soon as I have a date," she yelled over the enthusiastic crowd, "I will let you all know."

"Where, Mrs. McCain?" Pastor Collins stepped up to the pulpit and the crowd fell silent. "Will you be needing the church for the performance? I assume so?"

"Yes, if it's all right with you. There's not really an appropriate place other than here."

"I'm delighted to offer you the use of it."

Noble flicked the reins to get a little more speed out of the horses as he drove them across the moon-washed prairie. Beside him, Gracie was still grinning like a mule eating briars. She was beautiful when she smiled and the reception to her idea of a show had put a glow about her that was magical.

"You're pretty excited, aren't you?"

She laughed. "Oh, yes. I can't stop smiling. I know it's not a big show in New York, but it will be so much fun, and the children will love it. It's just…it's just wonderful." *To have someone believe in me.*

Noble chewed on his bottom lip and ran some numbers through his head. "You need time to pull together a show that will really *wow* Last Chance."

"Oh," Gracie shrugged. "I'd love to put something complicated together with sets and maybe other actors, but there's no time. We need to buy seed."

"Well, I had an idea about that."

"I'm all ears."

"Mr. Weatherspoon was there tonight. He saw the interest. I'd be willing to bet he'd sell me the seed I need on credit. We could pay him back with the proceeds from the show. In fact, I think we can pay him back and you'll still make money. But I could be wrong. I don't know the theater business like you do."

"Everybody in town is going to come to your show," Matt said from the back. "Mrs. Taylor said there are seven hundred people in Last Chance. That's a lot of pennies."

Noble quickly did some rough math and the numbers were good. Gracie didn't even need half the town to show up to make the seed money. "'Course, I suppose it depends on expenses."

"They shouldn't be much." She used her fingers to tick off a list of items. "I have odds and ends for costumes. The church shouldn't cost anything. I assume my helper"—she cut her eyes at Matt— "will be volunteer. Possibly some small expenses for props, but—no, expenses should be minimal."

"I think you should start planning the show—a real show. Pick a date and get the word out."

15

It was Noble's turn to be nervous. He wiped sweaty palms on his thighs as he and Gracie strode toward the feed and seed.

He had a good idea of what he wanted to plant and where. The plowing was nearly done. He needed the seeds in the next few weeks, if not sooner. He'd prayed, prepared a speech for Mr. Weatherspoon full of numbers covering acreage and yields, and had Gracie with him to reinforce the enthusiasm for her show.

He prayed again under his breath as he held the door for her and they entered the musty, dark building that smelled of hay, burlap, and molasses. Bags and bags of feed, seed, and fertilizer were packed up to the rafters. The rumble of the mill filtered from the back of the building. Noble let the door go and scanned the building, hoping to see Mr. Weatherspoon and not his shallow daughter, Jillian.

He breathed a sigh of relief when the door jangled shut behind them and a man's voice came from beyond a stack of seed bags. "Who's that?"

"Noble McCain. I'm looking for Mr. Weatherspoon."

"You found him." A short, round fella with an impressive beard and sideburns poked his head out from behind the feed. His face lit up immediately. "Mrs. McCain." He hurried toward them, hand extended. "What a pleasure, what a pleasure," he said, his Southern accent thick and heavy. He shook their hands and Noble's confidence increased. The man was obviously glad to see Gracie. "What can I do for you folks?"

"I'd like to talk a little business. Now, I know you don't know me or Mrs. McCain real well—"

"I reckon I know you well enough." He winked at Gracie. "How can I be of service?"

They had not planned it this way, but Gracie jumped in and made the request. "We were wondering if you could see your way to giving us a little seed on credit, Mr. Weatherspoon," she said, sounding a little rushed. "We'd pay you back before harvest with the money from the show I'm going to do for the town."

Mr. Weatherspoon smiled kindly, almost fatherly. He took Gracie's hand between his. "Mrs. McCain, the bracelet you returned to my daughter is worth a small fortune. You have proven your character to me." He looked up at Noble. "Both of you. You have credit with me for whatever amount you need."

NOBLE GLANCED over his shoulder at the wagon full of seed and feed. It seemed everything had happened so fast. Mr. Weatherspoon had practically thrown credit at them. Noble, however, had been conservative, not anxious to go into any unnecessary debt. The whole thing had been easier and faster than he could have imagined, and he was grateful. He glanced up at heaven, though, with a scowl, because he was also annoyed.

"Funny, isn't it?" Gracie said from beside him.

"What?"

"Oh, just the way things work out sometimes. If I hadn't pilfered the little princess's bracelet, I wouldn't have had anything to return to her, and her father wouldn't have known you from Adam's house cat." She crossed her arms over her chest and raised her nose in the air, clearly pleased with the turn of events.

"It doesn't bother you that he gave us the credit based on a lie?"

"What lie? So maybe my character is a little iffy. Yours definitely isn't. I returned the bracelet because *you* made me. You're honest and hardworking and you didn't take advantage of all the credit he wanted to give you. Which further proves your character. So, you should just accept it. It worked out."

He ran his tongue over his teeth, still dissatisfied with the situation. He couldn't shake the nagging feeling he should have told Mr. Weatherspoon the truth. He hadn't because of the embarrassment it would have caused Gracie. *I'm sorry, Lord. Forgive me if I've done the wrong thing here. Telling the truth or protecting her?*

He sneaked a sideways look at her. She wasn't sorry for stealing the bracelet. That bothered him more than anything. But then, maybe Gracie just didn't know what she didn't know. "God's Word says thou shalt not steal. And we're also commanded not to lie."

She looked down at her hands, absently flicked her thumbnails against each other. "I'm not a thief. I didn't like you calling me one, either."

He had been harsh that Sunday. He'd spoken the truth but not in love. More out of embarrassment. His wife—a woman of questionable moral character, stealing jewelry at *church*, of all places. He pulled off his hat and wiped the moisture from his forehead. "I'm sorry. I was pretty angry with you."

"I didn't say you weren't right. I just didn't like hearing it from you." She trailed off there at the end, but he'd heard her. And he didn't know what to make of it. Or how it made him feel. She valued his opinion of her.

Maybe that was good. Maybe he could share the gospel with her, lead her to the Lord. He just needed to practice some patience with her first. "It's over and done. We'll move on."

He'd try to forget Mr. Weatherspoon had acted generously based on a lie, but it sure stuck in his craw.

THE NEXT MORNING, without telling Gracie, Noble headed right back to town, but took Matt with him for company, and to share a moral lesson with him.

"I don't understand, Pa. You need the seed. And you didn't lie to Mr. Weatherspoon. I agree with what you said Miss Gracie said. Your character is good."

"That's exactly why I'm taking the seed back. I knew the truth—the whole truth—but let Mr. Weatherspoon believe a lie. It's the same thing as lying when you misrepresent things, son."

Matt tugged on his ear and frowned in a bewildered way. "I guess I understand. I understand Miss Gracie's point, too, though. And you're always quoting that Scripture that God works all things for good. Didn't He work what she did to your good?"

"God won't bless things that make you complicit in a lie. He'll give you the choice. I've made mine."

A few minutes later, they pulled up in front of the feed store and Noble locked the brake. "Don't get in any trouble and be back here in half-an-hour."

Noble found Mr. Weatherspoon in his office. Smiling warmly, the gentleman came from behind his desk to shake hands. "Mr. McCain, back so soon? You need to add something to your account?"

"No, sir, that's what I came to talk to you about."

Mr. Weatherspoon's brow dove, perhaps over Noble's dour expression. "Have a seat."

Noble obliged and fidgeted with his hat in his hands. He didn't know what he was going to do without the seed, but they'd figure it out.

"Now, what's this about?"

"Mr. Weatherspoon, Gracie stole your daughter's bracelet. I made her give it back. I didn't want to tell you yesterday because I didn't want to embarrass her, but I can't take your credit, your seed, or do business with you at all under a lie. I brought the seed back. Didn't even unload it."

Mr. Weatherspoon's whiskered jaw fell open. He blinked after a moment and closed his mouth. He seemed to then get a handle on the information and laced his fingers together on his desk. "Why? Why did your wife do that?"

Noble searched for the answer. He still didn't know everything about Gracie he needed to know, but he had a good guess. "I think she made her living for a while surviving the best way she could. And then she married a man who didn't know the Lord and he—well, didn't guide her."

Mr. Weatherspoon tapped his index fingers together, nodded his head slightly as if having his own internal conversation. "Mr. McCain, perhaps I was wrong about your wife, but I wasn't wrong about you. There's no need to return the seed. You have an open account here. Use it as you need."

"Are you sure? I mean, thank you, but—"

"I can name a dozen people who have accounts with me right now…who aren't as honest as you. And I'll tell you something else…" He leaned in. "I heard about your wife entertaining Betsy down in the mercantile the other day. Maybe she's still pliable, Mr. McCain. Maybe the Lord is working with her. A Godly husband can bring out a lot of good in a woman. Be a clear example to her. She might surprise you."

"Yes, sir. I sure hope so."

They shook hands and Mr. Weatherspoon came around his desk to get the door. Upon pulling it open, Jillian nearly fell into the room.

"Oh, Father," she said, straightening up and brushing down her shirtwaist. "Mr. McCain. I'm sorry, I didn't realize you had someone in here."

"I was just leaving." Noble nodded, well aware the girl had been eavesdropping. "Mr. Weatherspoon, thank you again."

"Certainly."

Noble didn't smile at Jillian. "Ms. Weatherspoon." He hoped his eyes shared his disapproval of her conduct, regardless of how oblivious her father seemed.

"Come in, Jillian, my princess. What did you need?"

The door closed behind Noble and he *tsked* at the man's blind spot for his daughter. No wonder she was so mischievous. A hellion with no hand to guide her. He dropped his hat into place, glad the girl wasn't his problem.

16

The one thing Melvin had exceeded at was utilizing the space in the wagon to a genius degree. From hidden drawers to pocket doors to narrow closets, there were things hidden in this wagon even Noble and Matt didn't know about.

Two of her prized items had been tucked away for safe-keeping and now she pulled them out, one by one. Her carefully crafted puppets—Belle and the Beast, resided in a secret compartment in the floor. She freed the marionettes from a burlap bag and lovingly caressed the bright yellow hair on Belle. Big, round blue eyes blinked from their counterweights as she inspected her. Belle's dress, an ornately tailored gown done in blue silk and covered in satin bows would delight every little girl in town.

The Beast, on the other hand, was quite the sight. A hairy cross between a bear and a wolf in a red uniform. So ugly, yet Gracie had always been enthralled by his heart. Tender, kind, wanting to be more than he was, but harshly judged because of his appearance.

She'd always felt more of a kinship with him than Belle. Cursed to live a dark, lonely life, he'd eventually given into it and surrendered the hope for anything better…until Belle came along. Pretty, sweet, determined Belle.

Gracie set the Beast aside and picked up the female puppet. She stood and carefully grasped the main bar from which all the strings ran down to the puppet. With her left hand, she tugged on the leg strings and Belle did a little kick. Pleased with the condition of the puppets, Gracie laid them on the bench, and then loosened a latch in the ceiling.

Carefully, working to avoid a blow to the head, she released the end of a door that swung down like an attic door. The board, upholstered in burlap, was covered with a few of the play props Gracie had managed to hang on to over the years. A feathered mask with a wooden handle, a pair of velvet slippers, and the costume from her part in The Comedy of Errors, an intricately embroidered, red and gold silk gown styled for sixteenth century England.

"Oh, there you are, my beauty," she whispered as she ran her hand over it. Melvin had come up with the idea to glue burlap to the board and then pin her costume items in place. And it had worked. The props looked like new. She had no doubt the gown would get a gasp from the country folk in Last Chance.

The rumble of a wagon interrupted her musings and she peeked out the window. Sheriff Darcy and Jillian Weatherspoon were riding into the McCain Homestead. Annoyed,

Gracie closed the board back into the ceiling, hooked the latch and hurried outside.

Noble and Matt stood side by side, waiting on the visitors. Only, something told Gracie this wasn't a social call. The tense stares from the occupants of the wagon aimed at the McCain men kept her on the stoop.

"Sheriff," Noble said as the lawman stopped the wagon and set the brake.

"Mr. McCain, I'm sorry to say I'm here on account of your son."

Gracie gasped.

"What's the trouble?"

"Some boys broke in to the feed and seed, stole some tack."

Noble turned to Matt. "You know anything about this?"

"I saw him there," Jillian said, pointing an accusing finger. "As the boys were running away, I saw them with the tack, and he was at the rear. I'm sorry, Noble."

Noble? Something hard and sharp squirmed in Gracie's guts.

"I didn't have anything to do with this, Pa."

"You calling Miss Weatherspoon a liar?"

Gracie strode over to the group. "Did you see him with any of the merchandise, Jillian?" She didn't know what had happened, but she would have bet her eye teeth Matt hadn't stolen anything.

"Not in his hands, no…" She shifted uncomfortably. "But I saw him there."

"Outside your store?"

"Yes."

"Uh-huh. But you didn't see him with the tack?"

"Well, no. But I've seen him with those boys."

"He could have simply been standing outside, minding his own business when they went running by." Gracie turned to Matt. "What's your side of this?"

"Thanks for asking." He shot his father and Ms. Weatherspoon quick glares and then addressed the sheriff. "I was looking for my friends. Usually find them in that back alley behind the feed and seed. The boys came running past me like their tails were on fire, so I ran, too. Only, I had to meet Pa at the mercantile, so I turned up the alley between the mercantile and the bakery."

"The boys. Your friends?" the sheriff said. "You saw them come out of the feed and seed? Did they have any tack or anything in their hands?"

Matt thought for a second and shook his head. "They were running so fast, I couldn't tell anything or anybody."

"You're lying," Jillian snapped. "That boy Bartholomew took a new bridle and reins with some conchos on them."

Noble stepped up. "I'll thank you not to call my son a liar, Miss Weatherspoon."

"I am telling the truth, Pa. I was leaning on the building. These boys ran behind me so fast I thought a bear was after them. When I didn't see anything chasing them, I took off anyway. I don't even know if Bartholomew was there."

The sheriff sighed and scowled at Jillian. "His version is a little different from what you said in town, Miss Weatherspoon."

"Well, I..." she worked her mouth back and forth, bounced her gaze around the group. "I could have been mistaken. I was so sure he was with those boys."

"Matt." The sheriff tapped his badge. "Don't make me come out here again. Stay away from Bartholomew and his buddies."

The boy nodded. When the wagon was out of sight, Noble sighed and turned away, scrubbing his face with a weary exasperation. Matt and Gracie exchanged tense glances.

"I'm sorry, Pa, but I really didn't steal anything."

"The Bible says bad company corrupts good manners. I've tried to impress that on you. Now do you see?" He swung back to his son. "You were basically guilty in Miss Weather-spoon's eyes just by association."

"She sure was quick to come after me, even though she said she saw Bartholomew, too."

Gracie found that point interesting.

"Maybe that's because she got the best look at you and not him, seeing as how you were bringing up the rear."

Matt settled back a little and didn't argue.

"You're feeding the livestock morning *and* night for the next week. And you won't go into town until I say."

Matt kicked at a stone. "Fine."

"I'm going for a ride." Noble stomped past them headed to the barn.

Gracie considered her next words carefully and walked up to Matt. The boy seemed to take advice from her a little better than his own father. "Now you know."

"Know what?"

"Arrow-straight, honest, and sincere. None of it matters if your friends are thieves."

He kicked at the ground again. "I guess neither one of us is doing Pa any favors."

The comment stung. "What do you mean?"

"Pa tried to give Mr. Weatherspoon back his seed. He told him the truth about the bracelet you stole."

"But Noble still has the seed."

"Mr. Weatherspoon wouldn't take it." Matt tilted his head, seemed to consider the situation, as if he couldn't quite understand all the ins and outs of it.

"Your father is a good man, Matt." Gracie felt a little sad and confused. Why hadn't Noble told her he was going to take the seed back? Because he was ashamed of her? And now this mess with Matt. "You're right, we're sure not doing him any favors." She slapped him on the shoulder. "Let's do better."

17

"Mrs. McCain, Mrs. McCain!"

Gracie stopped on the boardwalk and turned into the flow of oncoming pedestrians. A few men tipped their hats at her as they approached but she saw a hand waving at her behind them. Mr. Purcell pushed through a group of women with apologies, and raced toward her, an envelope in his hand.

"How fortuitous. I was just about to ride out to your spread."

"Mr. Purcell, nice to see you. What can I do for you?"

He glanced around and then pulled her over to the window of the bakery. "Ever since the town meeting, where I saw the reaction of Last Chance to a theater, I haven't been able to get your idea out of my mind. And then…they found the remains of the men from the hunting party."

Gracie winced. "Yes, the sheriff was out at our place this morning. He brought me some items that belonged to Melvin." She wished his loss had affected her more, but she saw no reason to fake grief she didn't feel. She'd merely placed the watch, the tie clip, and the double-sided coin in a small box and tucked them away in one of the hidden drawers.

"I'm sorry. It seems we're grieving the losses all over again."

Yes. The pain was palpable for some people here in Last Chance. She wasn't one of them.

"I believe this makes your theatrical production all the more important for the town and I have a proposal for you."

"All right."

"I'd like to turn my furniture store into a theater. And I'd like half the proceeds from any of your productions."

Gracie took a step back. This was so unexpected, she couldn't think for a moment.

"I've done my research, Mrs. McCain. Fifty percent is very generous, since I will be absorbing the cost for refurbishing the store into a theater. I want to work with you, have you involved in the redesign, so it's done nicely but not too much. The theater, the way I see it, can grow with the town. Last Chance needs this. What do you say?"

Gracie had to admit the offer was generous. Most theaters took seventy-five percent of the box office. "Would you stick to the agreement for three years?"

"Three? I was prepared for two." Mr. Purcell pressed a finger to his cheek and looked heavenward. After a moment, he nodded. "Three it is."

Gracie offered her hand, and they shook on it. "Last Chance has a theater."

"And I'll have the papers for you in a day or so."

. . .

"I have some news."

All of their plates full of corn bread, beans, and bacon, Gracie sat down, folded her hands and closed her eyes. Noble was a little startled by her declaration *and* her simple acceptance that nothing came before the blessing. There were moments here he felt as if he were raising two children.

Sharing a quick, amused smile with Matt, they bowed their heads. "Um, Lord, thank You for this day. Thank You for all the planting we've accomplished so far. As always, may we be grateful for every meal, and please bless the hands that prepared it. In Jesus's name we pray. Amen."

He and Matt looked up at Gracie. She was alight with some news that, judging by her nervous, adorable smile, had to be good. As long as it didn't invite another visit from the law, Noble thought he could muster up some interest. "We're in suspense."

"Mr. Purcell has offered to renovate his furniture store and turn it into a theater. He only wants half the profits for the first three years."

"Half?" Noble said, alarmed at the amount.

"You don't understand. Theaters typically take seventy percent of a show's box office receipts. Fifty percent plus the renovation is generous."

"Oh." Noble nodded, feeling better about the offer. "Guess I have a lot to learn about the business." He pushed some beans around his plate, trying to figure the implications of what was happening here. "Sounds like you might be getting your theater sooner than you thought."

"Sounds like."

Something about this made Noble feel…a little down. He couldn't put his finger on what was bothering him exactly.

Perhaps it was his silence or lack of exuberance that Gracie read as a negative. "I made a deal with you two." She smiled at them both. "We've got crops to plant and farm chores. I can do a lot of what needs doing in the evening or perhaps on Saturdays, if you wouldn't mind."

Mind? Noble didn't feel like he had any right to say one way or the other what Gracie could do with her time. This was a business arrangement. She had staked the farm. Got him the credit for more seed because of this theater thing. And, clearly, the town was eager for some entertainment. Maybe the theater would wind up helping the farm get started, rather than the other way around.

"We'd appreciate as much help as you want to give, but I think your theater project is important, too, judging by the way the town reacted to it."

A pretty blush crept up her cheeks and she pulled a strand of golden hair around to twirl in her fingers. A shimmer came into her eyes that touched his heart, and she nodded at him. "We'll figure it out."

GRACIE WAS STILL STUNNED. She ambled down the boardwalk oblivious to anything but this amazing, unexpected change of fortune. Mr. Purcell's offer—now in writing—changed everything. A stage. Houselights. The potential for the production shot up like a Chinese rocket.

And Noble supported the endeavor. Perhaps the most stunning or at least most difficult development to comprehend. His support mattered tremendously. He made her feel…valued.

But she couldn't do this alone. Matt was definitely going to have to help. She wanted to ask Noble to be involved, but she didn't see how he could spare the time away from farming. If not, who?

If just one more person, preferably someone with even a little theater background would come on board with this project. What about Faith? Or Heather? Oh, but they were ridiculously busy, too, and Gracie hadn't made the effort to get to know them. Now she regretted not having reached out to more ladies in town.

"Mrs. McCain, I got your answer." Faith burst up on the boardwalk and grabbed Gracie's hand. "I was just about to rent a buggy and come find you."

Gracie's heart leapt. "An answer to my letter?"

"Yes, yes." Faith was fairly shivering with excitement. "You won't believe it."

"But first, I have to thank you, Faith. You gave me the idea to try to do a show of some sort and Mr. Purcell has offered to renovate his furniture store into a theater. A real theater for the show."

"That's wonderful news. Oh, my, Last Chance is moving up in the world. Well," she tightened her grip on Gracie's hand and turned to go. "Come with me and see your surprise. It might be just as welcome."

"My surprise?"

The ladies rushed past the livery, crossed the intersection at the depot and stormed up on Faith's porch. Gracie couldn't imagine what had the woman so excited. Obviously, Stacy had received her letter. Had she sent a gift?

Faith flung open her door and waved her arm. "Ta-da."

Puzzled, Gracie stepped in and gasped in shock.

Stacy Medlin rose from the settee and smiled with her bright red lips. "Hello, Gracie."

Some people could make an impression on a room just by entering it and Stacy Medlin was one of those people. A buxom, shapely, beautiful woman, she carried herself like an empress. Cinched into a tight, emerald green dress, it matched her eyes perfectly and set off her fiery red hair, which was piled high in the latest fashion. Gracie had always thought when someone thought of an actress, they should think of Stacy.

The two of them clutched hands and Stacy kissed Gracie's cheeks. "It's so wonderful to see you after all these years."

"You haven't changed a bit. In fact, I think you're more beautiful."

"Oh, stop it." Stacy waved off the compliment and batted long, thick lashes at Gracie. "You're embarrassing me."

A thing which, Gracie knew, was not possible. "But what are you doing here? I told you it would be a while before I was putting a show together."

"I was passing by and, thought, what the heck, I'll stop in."

The two of them hugged. "Oh, I'm truly delighted to see you. It turns out your timing might be more fortuitous than I had planned, but I can't put you up. You'll have to stay in the hotel. How are you set?"

Stacy winked. "In clover. I just finished six weeks at the Adelphi and I'm on my way to San Francisco."

"Oh, well…" That explained the new dress and high-end hair style. "Congratulations. Um, why don't we get you settled at the hotel—"

"Already done. I came to see your lovely little post-mistress," she motioned to Faith, who had moved behind her counter and was listening intently, "who offered to get a buggy and help me find you."

"Thank you, Faith. Your help has been so appreciated."

"My pleasure."

"Come now, Gracie," Stacy hooked her arm around Gracie's and led her to the door. "Let's spend some time catching up…Oh, thank you, Mrs. Thornton."

Faith nodded.

Gracie let Stacy lead her, but said, "All right, but I have something to show you."

• • •

STACY PRESSED her forehead against the glass and squinted through a hole in the newspaper. After a moment, she cut her eyes over at Gracie. "It's small." She straightened up and patted her hair. "Although I suppose Last Chance is small as well."

"Come inside."

One of Mr. Purcell's crews had already made remarkable progress and Gracie was impressed. At the front, three men were sawing, hammering, and putting up the wall creating the lobby and ticket window. The ladies nodded politely at them and moved on into the theater. In here, two men were building the stage. "My, they are making progress quickly."

"Are they?" Stacy didn't sneer at the building, but Gracie heard the disdain in her voice.

"I have a reasonable expectation that we'll sell two hundred tickets."

"Really?" This news piqued Stacy's interest. "Why so confident?"

"Last September a blizzard killed dozens of men in this town. It has been a long, cold, dark winter. Everyone is ready for entertainment, for getting out and socializing. Laughter and inspiration."

"That is what the theater provides."

"Exactly."

"The building seems to be coming along." She smiled at Gracie and gave her a knowing, you-need-my-help look. "So, of what will your little show consist? And when is it?"

"On the 20th. My original thought was a puppet show and one, simple soliloquy. This, though," she motioned around them, "allows for more. I wish you were staying. You would be so much help."

Stacy turned and sashayed around the room, glancing at a sawhorse, lifting her hem out of some sawdust, and ending at the stage. "Your show is only two weeks away."

"I know the part I want to do, and I've done the puppet show a hundred times."

Stacy whirled in a flurry of lace and satin. "If this is a scam, it's too elaborate. You don't need a theater for what you want to do."

"That's because this is no scam." Gracie whipped a glance at the men working on the stage and pulled Stacy away from them. She dropped her voice and leaned in. "I'm legitimate now. I'll keep half the money and the other half goes to the owner. If you want to help, I'll pay you."

Stacy leaned back. "You're serious? I mean about this show being on the level?"

"Yes. Noble bought some seed on credit. We have to pay that back and maybe make some more improvements to the farm."

Stacy waved her hand and shook her head, as if this was too much to comprehend. "You're spending the profits on a farm?"

"Most of it, yes. The theater will be a slower project."

Stacy tilted her head and stared frankly at Gracie. "I think it's wonderful you want to go straight. And I want to help you. Free of charge."

"What? You don't have—"

"I want to. Oh, I'd rather see you take the money and run, but we can't spend our whole lives doing that, can we? At some point, we both have to settle down." She brushed a piece of sawdust off her sleeve. "Besides, I don't have to be in San Francisco for a month. Working with you will be like when we first started acting."

There had been a time in Gracie and Stacy's past, they'd lived off their grifting and their acting. Gracie didn't want to do that anymore, and maybe Stacy was changing her ways, as well. They wouldn't be young forever. But they both could act until they were too old to talk.

"Yes. Exactly. Acting," Gracie emphasized. "None of the larceny." But the day was wasting. "Oh, listen, I have to go. Noble is waiting on some supplies. And I am helping at the farm, but what about dinner tomorrow night? I'll bring my *family*."

"Your family. I would be delighted to meet them. And I'll give some thought to your show. How we can make it a real barn-burner."

18

Matt thought Stacy Medlin was about the most beautiful woman he'd ever seen. But at the same time, he wasn't so overwhelmed by her he didn't see something else. Something cold and insincere. She was pretty…but like a hard-packed snow drift.

Gracie introduced them and they all sat down to enjoy a meal at the Dawson Diner. They made a lot of polite small talk. Pa was always good at keeping a conversation going, but the truth was, his mind was back on a broken plow. Well, mostly back on the plow.

Matt wasn't stupid or blind. Out of boredom, he kept his head down during the dinner of chicken specials and light talk about the weather, crops, and goals for the farm. But a few times he looked up to watch the adults. He caught sight of his Pa giving, in his opinion, a couple of overly long looks at Miss Gracie. When he thought no one was looking.

Matt considered maybe he should be sad…but he liked Miss Gracie. He liked her…flaws. Ma and Pa had always been so perfect, and Matt felt like all he did was mess up, make Jesus mad. It was comforting, in a way, to see an adult try to figure things out, too, and make mistakes along the way.

Pa took his last bite and then dropped his napkin on the table. "Ladies, it's been a real pleasure. Matt and I haven't gotten out much in the last few years so this was a special evening. Unfortunately, I have some work I still need to do."

"Oh," Ms. Medlin bemoaned. "I'm sorry. You and Matt have been delightful companions. Must you go so soon?"

"Yes, ma'am. I broke a plow today. I need it fixed by first light."

"You'll be working all night?" Gracie asked.

"I hope not. But late."

"Well, I'll see you both before ten."

"All right. Good night."

GRACIE POKED at the remnants of her chicken, well aware Stacy was watching Noble walk away…and appreciating the view. He had a walk that was an enticing swagger, and the way his dungarees slid over his muscular thighs was something Gracie had noted once or twice.

When the door closed behind the McCain men, Stacy sighed dramatically. "Oh, my dear, Gracie, what a tall drink of water you have roped into a marriage. He is one handsome beast."

"I guess." Gracie cut a bite of chicken and lifted it to her mouth. "He's easy-going and pleasant to be around." *Most of the time…*

"And he has eyes for you."

Gracie's jaws froze. Both *what* Stacy said and *how* she said it reminded Gracie of the woman's skill in manipulating people. Usually, to cause trouble…or at least get something she was after.

Gracie swallowed the food. "I told you, it's a business arrangement and nothing else. You're imagining things. Or trying to cause trouble. Which is it?"

Stacy chuckled and threw her napkin at Gracie. "You're blushing. And I'm not trying to cause anything. Just an observation." She leaned forward and rested her elbows on the table. "Let's talk about the show."

MATT LIFTED his hat and shook out his sweaty hair. For April, it was hotter than a grass fire. He turned sideways to avoid an oncoming, barrel-chested cowboy who didn't give an inch. Probably because he was too busy looking at the gal on Matt's arm.

Beside him, Miss Medlin waved her handkerchief at her throat and sighed. "It's a hot one today. How much further?"

Somehow Matt had gotten volunteered to escort the actress to the telegraph office. The trip wouldn't be a total waste. While she was sending telegrams from Miss Faith's, he was going to scurry down to the mercantile and grab a root beer.

"Um, just right up here."

A few more steps and he opened the door to Miss Faith's. As he did, Miss Weatherspoon was coming out and nearly bumped into Miss Stacy. For a split-second it was like watching two cats meet for the first time, but the ladies quickly put on the fakest smiles Matt had ever seen.

"Excuse me," Miss Weatherspoon said.

"Entirely my fault." Miss Medlin stepped back and allowed the other lady to pass. They both cut their eyes at each other, as if trying to look without the other knowing. Matt did not understand this behavior at all and thought it was stupid.

Once Miss Weatherspoon was a few paces down the boardwalk, Miss Medlin moved. "I'll be a several minutes, Matt. You needn't wait but thank you for your most noble escort."

"Any time." He still had hold of the door and made sure not to let go until all of her hem and bustle was through the threshold.

Glad he didn't have to dress like a girl, he sauntered on down to the mercantile. Unfortunately, Miss Weatherspoon was in there and he hung back down the aisle of canned goods till she finished paying for some little doodad.

He purchased his root beer and ambled back out to the boardwalk, looking to his left. He really should hurry back to the theater. He'd been in the middle of sanding the stage when Miss Gracie had asked him to show Miss Medlin the way to the telegraph office.

"Who was your friend, Matt?"

Matt nearly jumped out of his skin at Miss Weatherspoon's silky, almost creepy tone. She was sitting on the bench, looking in the same direction.

"Uh, a friend of Miss Gracie's. She's an actress. I hear they go way back." Why was he running off at the mouth like this? Because girls made him nervous. He took a swig of his drink to get his bearings. "I gotta go. I'll see you later, Miss Weatherspoon."

He refrained from jogging—barely. The lady gave him the heebie-jeebies. Like a spider waiting on a fly. He was thinking about that and was about to turn down Grand Platte when he had the idea to play spy. Just for a little bit. Only as long as it took him to drink his root beer.

He turned back to go find and follow Miss Weatherspoon. For no reason other than to see if he could do it without getting caught and face his fear of her. He wandered around for about half an hour and was about to give up when he saw her come out of the telegraph office again.

And she was chatting with Miss Medlin. They turned his way and for a second his feet froze, but then he pressed himself inside the alcove of the saddlery and pretended to study a saddle.

"Oh, we go back further than I care to share, Miss Weatherspoon."

"So, you knew her before she married Mr. Erstwhile."

"Erstwhile? Oh…I'd forgotten his name. It's been several years since Gracie and I communicated."

"Why was that?"

"Just lost touch. Her husband had no love for the theater."

"What was it he did again? They came into town in a peddler's wagon."

"He peddled things."

"What kind of things?"

Miss Medlin and Miss Weatherspoon stopped suddenly, almost on top of Matt. He lowered his head a little more and tried to turn invisible. "Gracie's husband was a tawdry snake oil salesman. Which was why I so hated to see her leave the theater."

Matt got stuck on the word *tawdry*. He'd have to find a dictionary somewhere.

"But now she hasn't really left it, after all. Maybe being a farmer's wife hasn't agreed with her."

"Her first love has always been the stage. And after that incident in Abilene—Oh," the woman gasped. "I really should stop talking. I don't wish to be construed as spreading gossip."

But Matt had the feeling that was exactly what Miss Medlin was doing. Even more, pointing Miss Weatherspoon toward something.

"I won't tell a soul. What incident in Abilene?"

Miss Medlin shook her head. "Uh, uh, uh. You won't get another word out of me. I am the soul of discretion. Good day, Miss Weatherspoon."

Miss Jillian worried her bottom lip for a moment, but finally relented. "Fine. Nice chatting with you."

The women nodded at one another then Miss Medlin went one direction and, after exhaling a little huffy sound, Miss Weatherspoon went the other. Matt waited a solid minute till he moved.

19

Noble tossed the last bag of seed and two rolls of barbed wire in the back of the wagon and took a minute to catch his breath. He rested his arms on the wagon side and laid his head down for just a moment. The chores were endless. Always would be for a farmer.

But nothing beat watching what he'd planted grow. Even Gracie had squealed like he'd given her a present when he showed the corn sprouts.

Lithe, delicate hands landed on his shoulder and squeezed and massaged with an intoxicating rhythm. For a moment he lost himself in the feel of a woman's hands on his shoulders. It'd had been so long—

Shock arced through him and he spun. He'd hoped for an instant Gracie—but as the thought crossed his mind, he knew who the hands belonged to.

"Miss Weatherspoon." He stepped back like she might burst into flames.

She lowered her hands and donned a gravely sympathetic expression. "You looked so weary."

"Ma'am, I have attempted to avoid hurting your feelings, but I can see that was a mistake. I've no interest in any other woman than my wife." The thought surprised him that he was thinking of Gracie and not Jessie. "If you'd keep your hands to yourself, I'd appreciate it."

Miss Weatherspoon's face mottled almost purple and she clenched her jaw. "You are a fool, Noble McCain. That wife of yours is not who you think she is. She's some kind—some kind of huckster or grifter." Miss Weatherspoon clawed her way into the reticule on her wrist and snatched out a piece of paper. "Here, read this."

Noble hesitated but took the paper and unfolded it.

"I think she's here to rob the town," Miss Weatherspoon continued. "I think this play or show is a fraud."

Noble went deaf to her twangy, high-pitched voice. *Snake Oil Salesman and his associate caused ruckus here. Tonic they sold made half the town sick. Upon pursuing, they had disappeared.*

Sheriff Clem Davis, Atchison

Noble waved the paper. He was irritated with the girl, yet a sick feeling was growing in the pit of his stomach. "What does this have to do with Gracie?"

"I've five other telegrams that say basically the same thing. There was even a riot in one town."

Noble was almost speechless. "Do you realize how thin this is? There must be scores if not hundreds of snake oil salesmen in Nebraska alone."

"All of these hucksters had an associate."

"And?"

"Of small stature."

Noble used his hand to wipe the sweat off his upper lip instead of shoving this piece of paper into Miss Weatherspoon's mouth. "I'll thank you to keep these salacious and unfounded accusations to yourself."

"Surely you realize she was no saint. She stole my bracelet as easily as I take a breath."

Noble held his peace as there was nothing here to argue. And he did have to wonder if the snake oil salesman was the piece of her background Gracie was trying to hide.

"I told the sheriff all this," the woman spat, like an angry cat.

"And what did he have to say?" The slight tick in her brow answered the questions. Noble grabbed her hand and pressed the paper into her palm. "Miss Weatherspoon, mind your own business."

Noble slipped out to the barn after dinner to sharpen some tools and think. He'd been quiet at dinner and had tried not to be obvious about it, but suspected Matt and Gracie had noticed.

He snatched an ax off the wall and walked it over to the grinding wheel. *It's hard to keep up a good humor, Lord, when you're sitting there wondering if your wife has poisoned people.*

You could always ask her.

Yeah, just come right out and ask her if her husband was a snake oil salesman. A huckster. A grifter. And what part did she play in his pitches? Did she pick pockets? Relieve hard-working folks of their food money?

He settled in the seat, but paused with the blade on the stone. *It's a little hard to get past, Lord.*

Well, since you're without sin…

The thought brought him up short. He'd had some wild days before he'd settled down with Jessie. If not for her and her leading him to the Lord, who knew? He might have wound up a snake oil salesman himself.

"Noble."

Gracie's gentle voice, soft, hesitant, brought his head up. "Uh, yeah." He shifted away from her a little and then regretted the move, but he didn't think he could hide his concerns, and he wanted a chance to roll them around in his head a little more.

"I was walking the fields just now. I can't get over how fast everything is growing."

"Yeah, we're in good shape right now. Could use some rain."

"We have everything planted?"

"Just about. Another day or two. How's the show going?"

"Well. It's going well. Mr. Purcell had one of the carpenters build a collapsible puppet theater for us. And Stacy has been a godsend. She's hemmed a costume for me and picked a scene for us each to do."

"Matt's real close-mouthed about it. Says it's all a surprise."

She smiled, and he saw it out of the corner of his eye. She was so pretty when she gave those little half-grins.

"He's been such great help. I hope we haven't been away too much from the farm."

The kiss on their wedding day crossed his mind. Curling up with her on the bed on a cold, snowy day made his temperature rise. As did Jillian Weatherspoon's unwanted shoulder rub and how he'd wished it had been delivered by Gracie, instead. Aggravated by this train of thought, he scratched his head and put the ax back on its hook.

"Away too much? No. I'm a little surprised you've been able to get so much done." He stared at the wall, trying to think of something to do, but nothing came to him, except a question. "What about you, Gracie," he asked, turning to her. "How is life here in Last Chance working out for you?"

"I like it mostly."

"Mostly?"

"I spent so much time traveling around, that settling in one place makes me feel…vulnerable. Seeing the same people all the time. Knowing so much about them. And vice versa. That's been hard to get used to."

"They don't seem to know much about you at all." He pulled a bridle and reins off the wall, grabbed the oil cloth from a leather pouch and commenced to wiping down the gear. "You've been able to keep a lot your secrets, I think. Really, the trick is knowing who you can tell your secrets to. In a small town or a big city. You need people you can trust."

She drifted her fingers along Cyrus's stall, rubbed the animal's forehead when he came to see if she had a treat. "It's just that…well, what if those secrets…what if you just wanted to forget them?"

"Can you?"

She looked at him across the barn, in the fading twilight, her face falling into shadow. "I want to…so much. Never bothered me before. Where I've been, the way I lived. The things I've done." She meandered over to him and leaned a hip on the saddle stand. "Everyone here is so nice to me. I don't want to spoil that." She dragged her fingers lightly back and forth across the seat.

Noble set the tack down on the saddle, praying for the right words to help her somehow. He looked down at her, astonished at how small she was. In the wagon, they bumped into each other, maneuvered around each other. Scale was lost in the tight space. Out here, with nothing to measure her against, she was slight, petite, delicate. And she did seem vulnerable.

He rested his hands on his hips because they wanted to go to her face and he was glad for the saddle between them. "The way you find out who your friends are, Gracie, is by telling them the truth. It's like shaking a tree. Some people will fall away. Some won't. Those are the ones who will stick with you."

She stared up at him with burning intensity, as if his words were some new and great wisdom that she was weighing carefully. He clenched his hands, forcing them to stay put. How he wanted to caress her smooth cheek, pick up a strand of golden hair and feel the softness of it. Hold her again as he had that snowy morning.

She swallowed and stepped back. "Thank you, Noble. I'll...I'll think about what you've said."

She trudged slowly to the door, and then stopped. Silhouetted in the setting sun, she spoke over her shoulder. "Matt asked if I could teach him how to levitate a walnut. Would that be all right?"

"You can do that?"

She nodded.

He raked a hand through his hair, feeling as if they'd both let a moment pass. And he wasn't sure it was a good thing. But it was safe. "Sure. I don't mind. Just no card tricks," he said, lightening his tone.

He heard the smile in her soft reply. "No card tricks."

GRACIE LOOKED DOWN at her gown and smiled at the shock Last Chance would get seeing an actress in such a beautiful dress. Silky, satiny, flowing, bright red. Behind her, Stacy pulled the bodice a little tighter and stuck in a straight pin, wobbling the rickety footstool Gracie was standing on.

"This won't be a challenge. A little here and an inch at the hem and you'll be a beautiful Lady Anne."

"Can you imagine the faces when I come out in this?"

"These hayseeds will be picking their jaws up off the floor. But remember, the costume should never distract from the performance. Have you been practicing?"

"Yes, but Matt struggles. He reads well but the lines embarrass him."

"Well, what about Noble? That's why I picked this scene for you. So you could act with him."

Gracie was horrified, and then angry. "Still manipulating people. I knew it."

"Stop fussing. I was just trying to help things along."

Gracie would never even ask Noble to help. He was simply too busy with the farm. It was a nice idea, though. She resented Stacy's interference, but wasn't surprised by it.

"If he's not available, we'll ask Mr. Purcell. If he can't or won't do it, I'll read Percival's part from the wings."

Gracie chuckled and looked around the "wings." Two false walls separated the backstage area from the stage itself, with no curtain to cover the opening. For privacy, they'd borrowed a simple dressing screen from Last Chance's seamstress, Altar Laingsburg.

So, it wasn't New York-style, but it was a theater. And Gracie was putting together a production. Oh, a simple one, but a real theatrical production just the same.

She'd tell the fairytale Beauty and the Beast with her marionettes and Stacy, not surprisingly, was going to recite Lady Macbeth's soliloquy from The Scottish Play—as they most often referred to Macbeth. To say the name or quote from it in the theater if you weren't performing, brought a curse on the theater and the two actresses didn't want to invite any bad luck.

To close the evening, Gracie would perform the final scene from My Distant Love, a wildly popular British melodrama from a few years ago.

Stacy dropped to her knees and pinned the hem up. She spoke through three straight pins in her mouth, though she wore a cushion on her wrist. "You know, the whole town is positively giddy about this show."

"I know. It's exciting, isn't it?"

Stacy worked in silence until the last pin was used. "Gracie, you could walk away with the whole box office. The pews are in. You'll be able to seat two hundred people in here—"

"I'm not having this conversation with you again."

"We could go to San Francisco. I can get you a part in the play. You can give yourself another new name. Reinvent yourself."

"I'm tired of reinventing myself. I am Gracie McCain and I want to stay Gracie McCain." *If I can.* Noble had been trying to get her to tell him something the other evening. Her past. Spill it all. And she was too afraid. He was the one person she didn't want to shake and see fall away. Snake oil salesmen had such awful reputations. They lied and stole from innocent rubes.

"All right," Stacy sighed as she climbed to her feet. "I won't ask again. But, Gracie…" Stacy shook her head. "Your past could come calling here. What if someone recognizes you on the stage?"

"They won't. Everything I did with Melvin, I was in disguise. Always."

"Oh, well, that's fortunate."

A DEVIOUS LITTLE idea grew in Matt's head as he walked the knee-high corn. Pa was in the barn working on that stupid plow that kept breaking. Gracie was over by what they had taken to calling Hawk's Butte—just an outcropping of rocks the bird's liked 'cause it gave them a good view of the prairie. She was rehearsing her lines and the scene was so dang mushy Matt could hardly get through it with a straight face. He'd thought a time or two of asking her about Abilene, but something held him back. Besides, with all these stupid, romantic lines, another idea kept popping into his head.

What if Pa could be talked into saying those sweet, mushy

things? On the one hand, it was sweet revenge for all the times he'd been so perfect. On the other, maybe it would break some of the ice between him and Miss Gracie.

Somebody needed to do something. The way they looked at each other was becoming embarrassing.

Determined, he sauntered into the barn. "Corn looks good, Pa."

He looked up from the frame he was driving a screw into. "You finished already?"

"Nah. Just came in for a little water, and Miss Gracie asked if you had a minute. She needs some help." Matt's conscience barked at the lie. Well, it wasn't *exactly* a lie. She did need somebody to read the lines.

"Help? Did she say with what?"

Dang. He didn't know how to answer that without lying. "Well, no, she didn't say." And she hadn't. She'd just waved the script at him and said she'd be at Hawk's Butte.

Pa finished with his task and laid down the screwdriver. "All right. I'll go see what she needs. When I get back, we'll work on the cabin some."

They'd begun the project a few days ago. Matt, Pa had said, would have his own room by September. "Okay, sure."

Noble saw Gracie before he could hear her. She was standing in the shadow of the rocks and acting as if she were in a deep, intense conversation, occasionally waving her arms and pacing. She held a pencil in one hand and some papers in the other. Noble scratched his head beneath his hat and wondered if she'd had heatstroke.

"Gracie, you all right?"

She gasped and spun, her green dress swirling daintily in the emerald grass. "You're not Matt."

"No, he sent me out here. Said you needed some help."

"Oh, did he now?" Faux disgust tainted her features. "I guess anything to get out of reading his lines."

"His lines?"

He walked over and she passed him a slender booklet comprised of a handful of pages. "Mr. Purcell has agreed to play Lord Percival, but Matt was helping me rehearse."

Noble glanced over the script. Some pretty melodramatic words jumped out at him. No thirteen-year-old boy in his right mind would want to read this.

Noble held his arm out a little so he could focus on the words. "My darling, you have run from me long enough." He read haltingly, stiffly. "I shan't let you go again. We must end this charade here and now." Noble winced and looked at her. "Can you blame him?"

"It was a very successful play only a few years ago. When did you become a critic? I'm sorry if it's not as fascinating as the Sears, Roebuck catalog."

He huffed a breath. He'd hurt her feelings and she'd called him a hick, more or less. He hadn't come out here for trouble and she was working hard on the show *and* the farm. Not one complaint from her, either. Fine. "Well, I'm here and I have a few minutes. I can read as good as Matt."

"I wouldn't want to put you out."

"What would put me out is if I walked all the way out here for nothing."

Gracie crossed her arms, tapped her foot, but after a moment relented. "Fine." As if getting down to serious work, she took her hair, the pretty, golden mass of it, twisted it into a knot atop her head, and anchored it with the pencil. "I'll start at the top of page two. I'm having trouble there."

He flipped over, scanned the page. How hard could this be? "And what do I do?"

"You're Lord Percival. Follow along, read aloud when I get to his lines."

She cleared her throat, turned aside to him, and shrugged

her shoulders as if they were tight. "All right." She exhaled softly and passed a distant, melancholy stare out over the prairie. "It is maddening to be next to him every day. Pass him in the halls. Sit with him at the dining table. Watch him as he rides across the green hills. Yet he hasn't an inkling of my presence."

When the pause grew too long, he realized it was his turn. "Oh…I beg to differ, m'lady," he read flatly. "I believe Lord Percival is painfully aware of your presence in his home."

"He is as aware of me as one is of the downstairs maids or a piece of furniture in the corner." She sighed melodramatically and swept her arms toward the imaginary audience. "My heart bleeds a little every day, as his eyes pass over me. Never seeing me." She pulled her clenched hand to her breast and moaned. "I cannot continue on with this game. If I am not to be his wife, I would rather return to the fields of Lord Hemphill."

She is good, Noble thought. He could believe everything she was saying. Whoever this Lord Percival was, he was a fool. Impressed with her, he made his little pathetic attempt at acting. "Lord Percival and Lord Hemphill, will, I believe, both come to see your beauty and your kindness."

"Thank you, Daltry. I appreciate *your* kindness. I dare say Lord Percival does not know how fortunate he is to have a man with such dedication and loyalty."

"My lady…if you'll forgive me—"

"When you say that line, make a long pause after the word *turn*."

"Uh, all right." He scratched his eyebrow and started again. "My lady…if you'll forgive me for speaking out of turn…you are a fairer gift than either of them deserves. I would never waste your time here by ignoring you…if I were Lord Percival."

As he spoke in his flat, stilted way, Gracie's head came up and her eyes shone with interest. "You are forgiven, Daltry.

I'm only sorry Lord Percival does not share your keen insight. Very sorry, indeed."

Gracie turned to face Noble. She nodded at the script and he scrambled to find his place. "Um…my lady, I must confess, I am not Lord Percival's butler. Nor am I his servant."

"I don't understand."

"He asked me to spy on you. He thought you were seeing Lord Hemphill."

"Why on earth did he think that?"

"Forgive me, I beg you. I told him the lie."

Gracie gasped and stepped back. "What? Why?" She motioned subtly with two fingers for Noble to approach her. He took two, long steps.

"Closer," she whispered. "You have to take my hand."

He strode right up to her. Her gaze rattled his train of thought and he fought his way back to the script. "I have admired you from afar, Lady Ann." He took Gracie's hand, hesitated, then met her gaze again. His heart started pounding so fast and loud in his chest he believed she must be able to hear it. She was overpowering. He hadn't come out here for this. For her. Or had he?

"I…I wanted a chance to declare my love. Lord Percival isn't worthy to hold your hand like this, much less your heart."

Gracie's face went slack, as if she were shocked by something. The heat coming from their hands touching, their bodies simmering so closely together, brought sweat to Noble's brow. Gracie licked her lips. Fear and desire mingled in her hot gaze and he gulped, fighting down a desire that had roared to life in him like a lion. He tightened his grip on her hand.

"You're supposed to kiss me," she whispered. "You don't have to…"

Noble couldn't breathe. "I think I do." He needed to kiss her like he needed air. He cupped her cheek, pressed his lips to hers. This time there was no spark, only a force as powerful as a magnet, as hot as a volcano, as stirring as the touch of an angel. It forced the world away, a thousand miles. There was only Gracie and he pulled her into his arms, fighting the confusion of physical desire and the way he wanted so much more than her body.

Everything about Gracie, from her sweet mouth, surrendered and willing, to the feel of her pressed against him, was as right as rain. As right as soft, warm earth. As right as the way of things growing when he planted them. And he realized this had been growing since the moment he'd laid eyes on her.

Suddenly, Gracie backed away and her hands flew to her flushed cheeks. Her mouth was open in a scared little *o*. "I have to go to town. Thank you for helping me."

Gracie ran from him and he let her, because he was in the same shock she looked to be drowning in. He took his hat off and rubbed the tension in his neck. "What have I done, Lord, what have I done?"

GRACIE FLOUNCED DOWN BESIDE STACY, who was painting the finishing touches on a backdrop—the English countryside. The scene from My Distant Heart.

Stacy acknowledged her with a quick, sideways glance, but didn't stop painting. "If I didn't know better, I would say someone has been kissed. And kissed good."

"How do you know that?" Gracie was truly amazed.

Stacy backed away from the backdrop, waved the paintbrush thoughtfully at it, but seemed satisfied. "How?" She walked over to a worktable and set the brush in a jar of turpentine, then peeled out of the paint-stained smock. She scanned Gracie top to bottom and back again, shaking her head. "Much more and you'd be wearing a sandwich board with a heart painted on it."

"You're crazy."

"And you're a goner."

Gracie didn't like the way Stacy slapped on that label. As if she were irreversibly brainwashed or something. "You're not helping me. I came to ask for advice. I'm married to the man. I can't have these feelings for him."

Stacy quirked an annoyed eyebrow.

"You know what I mean. This was supposed to be a business arrangement."

Stacy sashayed over, stepped in face-to-face with Gracie. "You know what we'd do in the old days." Piercing, jade eyes challenged Gracie to face the answer.

"Run."

20

By the time Gracie returned home from town, Matt already had dinner started. He was tending to some meal in a Dutch oven hanging over the fire pit outside; biscuits were cooking on the lid.

"I'm running late," she said, riding by. "I'm sorry."

"No problem. Pa said he wasn't sure what time you'd be back." Matt tilted his head and squinted at her. "You and Pa have a fight or something?"

"No. Why?"

"He's acting funny. Quiet. Jittery."

"Oh." Gracie tapped her fingers on the saddle horn.

"Sort of like you," Matt added.

Gracie scowled at the teenage know-it-all and nudged her horse toward the barn. Noble was inside brushing the gelding down. She smiled nervously at him and led her horse, Cyrus, to his stall. "Thank you for putting Matt on dinner."

"Sure. I wasn't betting on what time you'd be back."

She'd very nearly not come back. Everything seemed to be spinning out of control here. She wanted to run from Noble… and run straight into his arms again. How the heck were they going to manage living in that little wagon now?

They had to talk about it. Surprisingly, abruptly, she found the courage to shake the tree. A little. "Noble, my name isn't Gracie Erstwhile."

He continued brushing, not even slowing down. "I kind of figured."

"It's Gracelyn Leah Walker."

"That's pretty."

"I haven't always been a very law-abiding person."

"I kind of figured that as well."

"Can people change?"

This made him pause. He rose up and rested his arms on the back of the horse. She loved the way the fabric of his shirt pulled tight against his broad, muscular shoulders. She loved the way his eyes were chocolate pools of kindness and patience. When he wasn't disappointed in her. She clenched her fingers to keep from moving a stray, brown strand of hair off his forehead.

"I believe people change when they get a real glimpse of God's love."

She wanted to yell she didn't know what that meant, but bit it back. Did that answer her question? Was she still flim-flam, tonic-huckster, pickpocket Gracie Erstwhile, or Gracie McCain--a woman with simple, honest ambitions? A goner. Could the wind blow her one way or the other?

I believe people change when they get a real glimpse of God's love. How does that help me? Answers that seemed as if they should be right in front of her…weren't. "He's so real to you, isn't He?"

"As real as you are."

"I don't feel real sometimes. I doubt He even knows who I am."

"He knows you. He knows everything about you."

"That's a terrifying thought."

"What's terrifying is that He loves you despite what He knows about you. I think that's what scares most people. I think when it comes down to it, the presence and love of a holy God scares the socks off them. It closes down their pride."

To be loved in spite of your flaws and failures was humbling. Being humbled was a frightening prospect. The right reasons—for love—at least gave it meaning. *Do You love me, God?*

She couldn't delve into this in front of Noble. Instead, she smiled weakly at him. "I'll go check on that dinner. It was smelling good."

AFTER DINNER, Matt and Noble excused themselves to the barn to clean their rifles. Gracie stayed on the wagon's stoop, practicing the puppet show, little Belle's dress floating elegantly as the doll danced.

Noble watched Gracie for a moment from the barn, then turned to his bench and started disassembling the Winchester. Beside him, Matt did the same.

They worked in silence for a few minutes. Noble was lost in a maelstrom of confusing emotions. He could kiss Gracie like that every day. Yet, he sensed the event had set them both back. Gracie more so. She was teetering. He didn't know how he knew, but she was thinking about running.

What do I do now, Lord?

"You look pretty dreamy-eyed, Pa. You want to 'fess up to

anything?" Matt smirked and shoved a cleaning rod down the .30-30's barrel.

"Nope, I do not." Noble's hands stopped. "I know you like her, Matt. I like her, too. More than I'd planned on, for sure, but I'm not sure it's a thing that will work out."

Matt's hands slowed but he kept working. "She's just like a kid, is all. One that wasn't raised right. I think between the two of us we can keep her out of trouble. We can—"

"I'm not convinced she's going to stay."

"You mean you think she's going to leave us?"

Noble pondered the question a moment then dove into cleaning his gun with determination. "I think it might be a possibility."

"But why? Wha—why?"

How could he explain to a teenage boy who'd never been in love how the emotion could terrify some people? Terrify them so much they ran from it. From the God who loved them…and people. "Just be prepared, is all I'm saying. And don't go saying anything to her. If she stays, it needs to be for the right reasons."

Matt huffed a deep sigh of disgust. "You grown-ups sure seem to go out of your way to complicate things. You like her. She likes you. I don't see what the problem is."

If only it were that simple…

21

Heather and Millie had their heads down and were whispering together outside the mercantile when Gracie approached. They didn't look up immediately and she heard Betsy's name whispered.

She was curious, of course, but it was none of Gracie's business to ask. "Excuse me, ladies."

Heather turned, gasped, and reached out, taking hold of Gracie's hand. "Mrs. McCain, we were just discussing the news about Betsy. Have you heard?"

A sinking feeling, like a rock plummeting to her stomach, rolled over Gracie, and she steeled herself. "No, what's happened?"

"They heard back from a doctor in Chicago who thinks he can help her—"

"Oh, that's wonderful news."

"Possibly. But it will cost Betsy and her mother a thousand dollars to get there, see the doctor, and stay at least a month. They don't have that kind of money."

Gracie's spirits plummeted. "That is a kingly sum."

"We have to do something," Millie said, her voice cracking. "She's dying."

"Dying?" Gracie felt the ground move. That precious, little girl…was dying? "Literally?"

Millie and Heather nodded slowly, their chins quivering.

Gracie backed away and turned from the ladies, unwilling to show her heart. "Excuse me." She wandered down the boardwalk, catching snatches of the ladies' conversation.

"Has to be something…

"We need…"

"Yes, a fundraiser of some sort…"

BEFORE SHE REALIZED IT, Gracie was at the theater. The show was only days away now. She noted absently the set for the puppet show was painted, assembled, and sitting in the middle of the stage. Mr. Purcell's men had brought in a dozen footlights and anchored them to the floor. Someone would need to light them before the show began. One more task to remember, Gracie thought in the back of her mind. In the front, her heart and thoughts were still on Betsy.

She blinked and brought herself back to the moment. The theater appeared to be empty. She didn't see any workmen. Didn't hear any noises coming from backstage. Troubled, feeling helpless, she sat down on the stage and looked around at the dark, open room.

She had an idea but couldn't imagine how to make it work out. Noble needed the money from the show to pay Mr.

Weatherspoon for the seed. They couldn't give it all to the girl and her mother.

But it would take it all.

"She can't be dying," she whispered. "Not her. She's just a child."

Gracie clasped her hands together and felt a plea—a prayer—try to escape, but she stopped it, blocking it with anger. God had no time to answer a prayer from a liar, a cheat….and a thief.

GRACIE'S REQUEST just about knocked Noble for a loop. He pulled back from their little dinner table and stared at her, barely resisting the temptation to stick his finger in his ear and clean it.

"What?"

"She and her mother need a thousand dollars to go to Chicago for a treatment that might save her life. I thought—I thought if there was any way we could give her the money from the show. I realize that puts you cross-wise of Mr. Weatherspoon, but if he knew, perhaps he would give you longer terms?" She sighed and stared down at her hands in her lap. "I just want to help her. I've never done anything good in my life."

Noble and Matt exchanged astonished looks. But the weight of Gracie's request, the heart behind it, finally settled on Noble. He reached over and took one of her hands. She looked up, surprise and hope in her shimmering eyes. "We'll make it happen, Gracie. If I have to give Mr. Weatherspoon our horses as collateral, we'll make it happen."

"You are a good man, Noble McCain."

He didn't like the way she said it. As if she were telling him…he was a saint. He squeezed her hand tighter. "It was your idea."

"But, like you said, you'll make it happen."

"Gracie, do you understand that everything good in me… is here because I want to reflect Jesus? I want to reflect His love."

"You're doing a wonderful job."

"You have an incredible capacity to love. Jesus just opens it up even more. When you realize how much He loves you…" He saw her expression change, darken, and he trailed off. She didn't believe He could love her. "Give Him time. He'll prove it to you."

She pulled her hand away and gave him a shaky smile. "Sure."

When Gracie took word of her donation to Millie, not only did it spread through Last Chance like a wildfire, it made Gracie something of a celebrity. Everywhere she went, people approached her, shook her hand, thanked her, said they couldn't wait for the show.

One afternoon, as she met Stacy at the front of the hotel, the sheriff walked up and greeted the ladies with a big smile. "I have to tell you, Mrs. McCain, I was profoundly relieved to hear about you donating the proceeds of your show to Betsy."

"Relieved?" Stacy asked, before Gracie could.

A little startled at her interruption, Sheriff Darcy bounced his gaze back-and-forth between the women. "Oh, you know how some folks are. Always looking for the bad side of things."

Gracie was puzzled by the comment, but again, before she could ask, Stacy seemed intensely curious. "How could there be a bad side to a simple theater production? Especially if it's a fundraiser?"

The sheriff chuckled and scratched his nose, almost like he was embarrassed. "Don't take offense, Mrs. McCain. One person in town has questioned your character. I bet if you thought real hard, you could figure out who." He winked. "You ladies have a good day."

As he walked on, Gracie ground her teeth. "Jillian Weatherspoon. That little wretch."

"More like a little detective, I bet." Stacy grabbed Gracie's arm. "Come with me." She pulled her back upstairs to her hotel room. "I have something to tell you that is important."

"All right, all right." Gracie pushed Stacy off her once they were in the room. "Quit pawing at me. What is it?" Now, suddenly, Stacy wasn't so eager to say what was on her mind. Gracie wanted to shake her. "Spit it out."

"Your last show. It was in Abilene, wasn't it?"

"Yes…how did you know that?"

Exhaling a weary—or melodramatic sigh—Stacy went to her nightstand and pulled a piece of paper from a slender, leather portfolio. Gracie remembered it from the old days. Stacy kept her scripts in it.

"Here."

Gracie took the paper and unfolded it. "Dear God."

She had to sit down on Stacy's bed before she fell down. A wanted poster screamed the words *Wanted for Murder*. Beneath them, a sketch of her and Melvin, and the likenesses were arguably very, very good. In fact, Gracie had been sketched as a woman.

For a moment she thought she might be sick. The man in Abilene, the one Melvin had knocked unconscious…had died.

Numb, stunned into silence, the poster slipped from her fingers. Questions hurtled at her like a rockslide. "Why didn't you tell me?" she finally managed.

Stacy came and knelt in front of her, took her hands. "Because you are my baby sister and I love you and I thought you'd be safe here."

"You weren't ever going to tell me?"

"No. I was going to leave you to your little theater, your

small town, and your handsome farmer. You deserve so much more than Melvin ever even tried to give you. I thought you'd found it."

"Then why did you encourage me to run?"

"I didn't encourage you. I wanted to see which way you might bend."

"But now. What do I do now?"

Stacy started to speak several times. Then she looked Gracie in the eye and said it flat-out. "The show must go on. But we're going to take the money and disap—"

"No." Gracie surged to her feet and moved away from Stacy. "No. I will not steal from this town." *Or Betsy. It would be so wrong. Worse, Noble would hate me…*

And, for the first time, she feared God might hate her.

Slowly, Stacy rose to her feet. "Gracie, I'm down to my last five dollars. There's a man in Chicago who is after me. If he finds me, he will kill me." Stacy's chin quivered. She wiped at the tears spilling from her eyes. "I got your letter. Last Chance sounded like such a safe, out-of-the-way place. And then you told me about your show. I knew it would be so wildly successful that you might see your way to giving me a few dollars…maybe even a place to hide. But, now, Gracie, we both have to run."

Gracie swallowed and fell back across the bed. She was too numb to cry, too crushed to wail in hopelessness. She stared up at the pretty designs on the tin ceiling tiles. Noble. Matt. She saw their faces so clearly.

Gracie McCain. Wife, mother…murderer.

One more time, Gracie Erstwhile would disappear. "We run, but we don't steal the money."

Gracie's throat hurt, like she'd swallowed a bandana, but somehow, she had to get through this dinner. She finished the bite of cornbread and smiled at the McCain men. "Gentlemen, if you won't miss me too much, I'm going to spend the night in town with Stacy. We're going to get an early start on a few things, and maybe do one more dress rehearsal before the show."

"I understand," Noble said softly, but then cheered up. "Everyone in town couldn't be more excited than if President Hayes was coming to Last Chance."

Matt laughed. "That sounds boring. I am curious to see how Mr. Purcell pulls off that part of Daltry."

"He's run through it with me twice. He's good."

Noble let a wry smile twist his mouth. "How good?"

Gracie couldn't muster a smile or a joke. She just felt as if she were lost in a gray fog. "Not as good as you." A look passed between them that electrified the air. "I should be going. Oh, the dishes—"

"I'll do them," Matt whined, sounding as if he were volunteering to cut off his arm.

"Thank you."

"I'll go saddle Cyrus for you…unless you need the rig."

"No, Cyrus will be fine."

A little sadly, Noble placed his napkin on the table and nodded at no one. "I'll see to it."

When he left, Gracie put her fork down. What little appetite she'd had was completely gone now. She only felt nauseated.

"You should give him a chance, Miss Gracie."

"What? Who?"

"Can't you see the way he looks at you? You look at him the same way."

"You're imagining things."

"No." He shook his head, not to be put off. "Pa's a good man, Miss Gracie. He's—"

"That's the problem. He is a good man." She slammed her fork down. "And you will be a good man, too, Matt." *If I get out of the way…* The knot came back to her throat and she tried to swallow it as she rose from the table. "I'm sorry. It's not your fault. None of this is your fault. Or his." She reached out and drifted her fingers across his cheek. "I'll see you tomorrow?"

He blinked like a bewildered owl. "Sure thing."

GRACIE LAID down on the bed beside Stacy and pulled the covers up. If she could get through the show tomorrow night, it would be her most magnificent performance. Maybe Noble wouldn't come and she wouldn't have to see his face in the crowd.

"I'll arrange for two horses to be ready tomorrow night." Stacy rolled over to face Gracie. "Saddled. Ready to go."

"Where?"

"I'll be out behind the livery waiting for you."

Like the old days. "Where do we catch the train?"

"Kearney. There's one at eight in the morning. We'll make it, but it will be close."

"And where are we going?" Gracie didn't know why she asked. She didn't care. It didn't matter.

"Let's shoot for San Francisco. I have employment there, remember?"

"Fine." Gracie rolled over and tried to sleep. Sleep didn't come. Her future was bleaker than she'd ever seen it. If they didn't steal Betsy's money, both she and Stacy were going to have to do some unscrupulous things to get anywhere, much less all the way to San Francisco.

God, if You're really there, if You really know me and love me, please show me a way out of this…

GRACIE ROSE EARLY and headed off for the theater. So many last-minute details to pull into place…for Her Show. Those words had made her so happy just hours before. Now, every time she closed her eyes, she saw that man in Abilene crumpled on the ground, Melvin with his hand raised ready to strike again.

She was no good. She'd been too long in a world where lies and truth wove around one another like snakes and somehow the lies always won, ruining anything good in Gracie's life.

She tried to expel the darkness with a long exhale, but it was pointless. Her heels clicked harder, louder on the board-walk, matching the hammering of her heart.

She drew up short, however, when Mrs. Johnson wheeled Betsy out of the bakery. The little girl was enjoying a cinnamon roll and laughing at the icing stuck on her fingers when she and her mother saw Gracie.

They smiled and waved, and Gracie had no choice but to speak. "Good morning. That looks like a scrumptious breakfast."

"It's very yummy."

"Are you excited about the show tonight?" Mrs. Johnson asked.

"Very."

"Everyone in town is talking about it. I'm sure it's going to be standing-room only." The woman pursed her lips, but a crinkled brow revealed her fight against tears. She blinked them back. "I can't say thank you enough. There's no way we'll ever be able to repay you."

Gracie knelt in front of Betsy. "You just get well. That's all the repayment I want."

"I want to give you something, Miss Gracie." Betsy handed off her sticky cinnamon roll, licked her fingers and then pulled something from her pocket. "I have kissed it with good luck."

In a clumsy attempt to recreate Gracie's trick, Betsy reached for her ear and came away with a mustache. "Holy cow, look what was in your ear."

"What?" Gracie acted astonished and took the hairy prop from the girl. "Oh, my goodness. And you say you kissed it with good luck?"

Betsy nodded enthusiastically.

"Well, then, I'll just have to get some of that luck to rub off on me." She pressed the mustache to her upper lip and wiggled it around.

Betsy chortled with delight and Mrs. Johnson grinned, the tears still shining in her eyes. Gracie stood and stepped back, proudly displaying the mustache. "Ladies, the theater awaits. I shall see you both this evening. Remember, you have seats on the front row."

Gracie strode on with forced cheer, head up, eyes straight ahead, ignoring all the amused looks, until she turned the corner and Betsy's laughter faded.

Then Gracie wilted like a flower in the sun. There was no way she could steal the money from Betsy. From Last Chance. Simply no way.

For a moment, Stacy looked as if she might have an apoplectic fit, right here, behind the room divider that created their little, rustic "dressing room." A tiny desk, a simple shaving mirror. Two short stools. Not grand but serviceable. Stacy spun away from the mirror to face Gracie. The flush in her cheeks, the tension in her face, it all suddenly fell away, and she relaxed, as if accepting the inevitable.

"All right." She took a calming breath. "All right. You can't steal the money. Then what is your plan?"

"I'm going to turn myself into the sheriff after the show."

Stacy's mouth fell open. She looked completely thunderstruck. A moment passed before she blinked. Then she closed her mouth and her eyes at the same time and appeared to be gathering her thoughts. Gracie knew this was hard for her sister to accept. Developing a moral compass had been a shock to Gracie, too.

"I don't mean to sound selfish…" Stacy opened her eyes again and they were wet with tears. "But what about me? I don't have the option of turning myself in. I'm not wanted for anything. The man who is after me will just kill me."

"Stay here. At least for a while."

"And do what?"

"You could run the theater. Noble is building a cabin. It's almost ready. You could live in my wagon when he moves into it."

"Your wag—" She bit that off, rose, and strode to the opening in the stage. "That's a very generous offer. And I think it's courageous of you to turn yourself in to the sheriff." She sniffled and turned to Gracie. "My sweet, little sister. You always had it in you to be a better person. But I'll be by your side when you give yourself up. To the sheriff."

Gracie was moved by Stacy's support. How often they'd fought like two cats. Over a man. Over a part in a play. Over foolish, foolish things that didn't matter. Stacy had always been so willing to do the most deceitful, treacherous things to get her way. Now, she had grown up and Gracie was glad she would have at least someone in her corner. "Thank you. That means a lot to me. I've no doubt I'll be a pariah when this gets out."

22

———

Noble took a seat on the front row at the end, saving one for Matt who was helping out by taking money at the door. Several folks in town greeted him, wished him well. He liked Last Chance, but it wasn't going to be any good at all if he didn't get things worked out with Gracie. He'd come tonight bound and determined to fix whatever was broken between them.

A thick, chubby hand landed on his shoulder and he looked back. Mr. Weatherspoon and a slender, gray-haired woman were sitting down behind him.

"My boy, Noble."

"Mr. Weatherspoon, good to see you." They shook hands over the pew.

"And you. Oh, I'd like you to meet my wife, Drucilla."

"Ma'am."

"And, of course, you know my daughter."

Jillian Weatherspoon sashayed down the space between the pews like a princess. And the smirk on her face…evil, satisfied. Noble half-expected to see a mouse's tail hanging from between her lips. She was wearing an I-know-something-you-don't-know look and it made the hair on the back of his neck stand up.

"Why, Mr. McCain." She extended her hand and Noble shook it, thinking he'd rather grab a rattlesnake. "I'm so very excited to see this production. I hear the ending is…quite the twist."

He didn't respond. Instead, he nodded at the family and turned back around. A few minutes later, Matt joined him, grinning wide and jittering like a Mexican jumping bean. "You wouldn't believe all the money, Pa. People have been making donations like crazy." His enthusiasm cooled when he saw Betsy at the end of the pew, sitting in her wheelchair. "I hope it's enough. She's a sweet kid."

Noble was proud of his son's compassion and squeezed his shoulder. "Me, too."

Matt settled back and punched Noble in the leg. "You ready?"

"I think so."

"You better do more than think."

"Why don't you let me worry about what happens tonight."

The rumble of conversation grew increasingly louder as more and more folks worked their way inside. Pews were full to bursting. People packed into them like sardines in a can. Men lined the walls, giving up their seats to women and children.

"Come on, we'll give up seats to the ladies, too." He and Matt headed to a spot against the wall, close to the side of the stage, in the shadows. A few minutes later, Mr. Purcell walked through and dimmed all the lanterns hanging over head. With the snuffing of each light, the volume on the conversation softened until nearly everyone was whispering. The footlights illuminated the puppet stage, painted up in vibrant colors, and reflecting lovely mountains and pastures. Gracie had said Miss Medlin painted it. Two talented women.

From where Matt and Noble stood, they could see the narrow ladder that led up to the puppeteer's walkway. Gracie had rehearsed this several times but had put most of her energy into that horrible, melodramatic scene from My Distant Heart. He was not aware of what Miss Medlin was doing exactly. Gracie had said she wanted to perform something from Shakespeare.

Once all the lights were down, Mr. Purcell walked to the stage. The muttering died to silence. "Ladies and gentlemen, I want to thank you all for coming to the inaugural performance of Last Chance's new theater and Gracie McCain's fundraiser for Betsy Johnson. Thank you so much for your generosity and support. I understand it has been overwhelming." He paused for thunderous applause. Mrs. Johnson reached over and hugged Betsy.

"Tonight," Mr. Purcell continued, tamping down the excitement, "we have entertainment for the children and the adults. From comedy to drama, from fairy tales to love stories, you are in for a treat."

As he spoke, Gracie climbed the walkway with her puppets and lowered Belle to the stage, the activity mostly hidden by Mr. Purcell's strategic position.

"Without further ado, please enjoy this rendition of Beauty and the Beast."

With a grand sweep of his arm, Mr. Purcell stepped out of the way. The audience gasped and chuckled at the little doll on strings wearing a flowing, blue silk princess gown—the stuff of little girls' dreams.

"Once upon a time," Gracie began, the puppet moving and gesturing as if it were narrating the tale, "in a castle, high on a cliff, lived a fearful beast…"

Noble listened to the tale, nodding and smiling, and like the audience, forgetting at moments the animated little marionettes weren't real. Gracie's voice was rich, strong, and full of emotion. She defined her characters perfectly and they moved with amazing life-like gestures. Overall, it was an enjoyable presentation. He was especially pleased when he glanced down and saw Matt's face—rapt with attention. The teenager, too grown up for such frivolity as a puppet show, was lost in the story.

When Gracie finished, the little theater erupted with applause, cheers, and whistles. She came down from the platform and stepped in front of the puppet stage, bowing with Belle and the Beast in her arms. The audience doubled its enthusiasm and she bowed several times. On her last one, she caught sight of Matt and Noble clapping and froze for an instant. An indefinable something in her expression told him she was pleased to see him. Them. Both of them.

Then a deep shadow of sadness colored her features as she turned away and headed backstage.

23

Backstage, Gracie quickly set the puppets down and jumped in to help Stacy finish lacing the back of her gown.

"Here, I've got this." She spoke softly so as not to be overheard by the audience.

Tonight, as Lady MacBeth, she would perform the famous sleepwalking scene. Stacy loved the part because, Gracie suspected, it appealed to her dark side. A woman intent on doing whatever it took to be successful.

"You've got your packed house out there, Gracie." Her voice was soft, husky. "And they sound like they were impressed."

"I think so."

"Betsy is going to get her trip."

From the stage, they heard the clatter and bumps of the puppet stage coming down and being stored backstage on the other side of the girls' dressing screen.

"Yes, by everything I've heard the money is pouring in. People have been very generous."

"And you said the sheriff would be counting it?"

"Yes, at his office."

The light in the theater changed and Gracie knew Mr. Purcell had lowered the footlights even more for Stacy's somber, eerie performance. A stagehand hired by Mr. Purcell propped up the backdrop she had painted.

"And now," Mr. Purcell began, "a scene from Shakespeare's play Macbeth. A story of murder and deceit. Of betrayal and blood."

"He's good," Gracie noted, tying the lace.

"Yes, he's becoming quite the showman."

"The prominent actress Miss Stacy Medlin will perform the part of Lady MacBeth."

Stacy brushed her dress smooth. Her long, red hair streamed down her shoulders. "How do I look?"

"Like an actress."

"At her insidious urging," Mr. Purcell projected, "Macbeth has murdered King Duncan, and the lady now deals with the deed in her sleep…"

"Go, go, go." Gracie pushed Stacy at the opening to stand behind Mr. Purcell.

"Her eyes are open," he finished, "but her senses shut." Once again, he swept his arm toward the stage and stepped aside.

Gracie watched for a moment. Stacy stood in the center of the amber light, head down, eyes closed. Then she began.

Breathing hard, body tense, she rubbed her hands frantically. "Yet here's a spot." She scrubbed madly at the fingers on her left hand. "Out, damned spot! Out, I say!"

Gracie grinned at the melodramatic performance but didn't have time to watch it all. She had to get ready herself and slipped back behind the dressing screen. The soliloquy wasn't very long, even with Stacy's emoting, and all Gracie had time to do was pin up her hair, pinch her cheeks, and fling on a red shawl.

As she was checking her face in the little mirror, the audience once more offered up thunderous approval, though without the many whistles this time. Not surprising. Shakespeare wasn't for everyone.

A moment later, after several bows, Stacy flounced behind the screen and hugged Gracie. "Oh, I love acting." She twirled once and then dropped into the seat in front of their mirror and looked at Gracie in the reflection. Suddenly, her expression sobered. "Gracie, are you sure? If you do this, you're going to wake up in jail. I say we take the money and run."

Gracie breathed a soft sigh and walked over to her sister. She clutched her shoulder and smiled sadly at her in the mirror. "There's a little girl out there who needs this money more than I deserve my freedom. Someone has to pay for that man's death in Abilene."

"Finally, tonight, my friends," Mr. Purcell said, "a lover's treat, I would say. A dip into the pond of romance and affairs of the heart. Mrs. Gracie McCain will finish our evening by performing the final scene from the stage play My Distant Heart."

Stacy patted her fingers. "Still going to tell the sheriff right after your performance?"

"Immediately."

"If it were done when 'tis done, then 'twere well it were done quickly."

Gracie nodded and walked out on to the stage.

Mr. Purcell stepped down and joined Noble over against the wall. He nodded subtly at the stage. "Knock 'em dead."

Noble hadn't been nervous until this very moment. Then it hit him like an icicle in the heart. He moved two steps closer to the stage but stayed in the shadows.

Gracie came out and paced for a moment, as if she were lost in her own world of make-believe, then stopped and passed a sad gaze over the audience. "What am I to do? My heart longs for him, yet he acts as if I am no more than a speck of dust on his windowsill."

Noble spoke from the shadows. "Lady Ann?"

She turned to the direction of his voice and Noble approached the stage but didn't step up. Gracie's eyes widened and her mouth moved but no sound escaped.

"Daltry, your servant, ma'am." A smile twitched on his lips but he fought it back.

Gracie blinked. "Yes. Yes, of course. Daltry. What are you doing here?"

Noble stepped up on the stage. "Lord Percival sent me to find you."

"Lord Per—" she spun away from him. "Not concerned for me, I'm sure. Perhaps curious as to why I was not at breakfast."

"Perhaps."

They went on through the little play and maybe Noble was no actor, but he sure knew how to kiss her for real. When he took her in his arms, he whispered, "If this is the only way I get to kiss you…"

Gracie melted to him and the audience went wild. Daltry, the underdog, had won them and the heroine over. They whooped, hollered, and cheered. After a moment, she tried to pull away. Noble fought her for an instant and then released her. He was shocked to see the pain in her eyes.

"I have to tell you something," she mouthed silently.

"Bravo," someone yelled from the crowd.

"Kiss her again, McCain!"

"Yeah, like you mean it."

Noble cocked his head at the rowdy the audience. "Again, you say?"

The crowd cheered and laughed and clapped wildly. Noble slid a mischievous gaze over to her. Gracie smiled and fell into his arms for a last, crowd-pleasing embrace.

24

Matt was rolling with laughter. He didn't know what was funnier: the stunned look on Miss Gracie's face when Pa had popped out of the shadows, or the way the crowd was egging them on for another kis—

Scowling like she'd just drunk tainted water, Miss Weatherspoon jumped up in the middle of all the chaos and was making a beeline for the back of the crowd. Matt took off after her.

Maybe she was just running to beat the crowd out of the building, or she was up to something else. He skidded to a stop half-way to the back. Through the crowd he caught sight of her waving a piece of paper in the sheriff's face. Really curious now, Matt hunkered down a little lower and wound his way closer.

"This is no joke. It's murder and it's her and that husband of hers."

Dour-faced, Sheriff Darcy took the paper from the grouchy woman and studied it carefully. After a minute, he nodded. "All right, Miss Weatherspoon, you get your wish. I'll talk to her after everyone clears out."

"You have to arrest her now, in front of everyone."

"No, I'm sorry. That's not the way this works. She's innocent until proven guilty." He leaned in a little closer and lowered his voice. "Let me do my job."

Matt scurried back to his place up front. Pa had just finished kissing Miss Gracie and, while she looked pretty flustered, she also looked a little sad. She whispered something to Pa, and he nodded.

The couple took a few more bows then Miss Gracie went behind the stage and Pa stepped down into the crowd. He disappeared from Matt's view behind a wall of townsfolk. Frustrated, he clawed his way through what felt like a hundred people all trying to clap his pa on the back and congratulate him.

Matt reached through the opening between a man's arm and his body and grabbed Pa's hand. "Pa, I gotta talk to you!" He yelled louder to be heard over all the good-natured ribbing and praises. "Pa!"

Noble scanned the faces, realized Matt had hold of his hand. "Uh, thank you, folks." He started pushing through them. "Thank you, I appreciate it. Save your compliments for the real star, though."

He managed to clear the group and let Matt drag him over to the wall. "Pa, I gotta tell you—"

"Mr. McCain."

The sheriff. Matt's heart shot to his throat and he yanked Pa's arm. "He's here for Gracie. You've got to get her out of here."

"What?"

As understanding dawned on Pa, the sheriff slipped a piece of paper in front of him. In the faint light, Matt could see the letters through the backside.

Wanted.

"Gracie, may I come back?"

She turned away from the mirror to the dressing screen. She could see the top of Noble's head over it. "Please."

He stepped around it into the little space and sat down. Gracie thought he looked as sad as she felt. Would he come visit her in jail? Was that a ridiculous hope?

"Thank you for being in the play. Why did you do that?"

"I would have thought that might be obvious."

Obvious? What? That he cared for her. Could he…if he knew the truth?

"I have to tell you something." She wasn't running from any of this anymore. The only hope she had was that he and Matt wouldn't hate her. She wouldn't dare dream of more.

"I'm listening."

"My husband was a snake oil salesman…and everything that means. We did awful things. Sold tonics that made people sick. We lied to them, stole from them. I'm sorrier than I can say. I've wanted to tell you the truth so many times…tell you everything."

"And what is everything?"

"I'm going to turn myself into the sheriff."

His face went slack. "For what?"

She exhaled a long, sad breath but she wasn't going to

stop now. "Stacy told me something a few days ago. Oh, it's awful, Noble. You're going to hate me but I have to tell yo—"

Gracie's thoughts skidded to a stop. And then pieces of a puzzle fell into place like bolts of lightning. Stacy's desperate attempt to get Gracie to steal the proceeds. Her concern over nosy Jillian Weatherspoon. The wanted poster. Making sure Gracie was going to have the sheriff occupied after the show.

"Tell me what?"

Gracie surged to her feet and Noble followed. Surely, Stacy wouldn't…only she knew her sister. Stacy would. "She quoted the Scottish Play."

"What?"

"Noble, I don't have time to explain. Just trust me. Please. Go to the sheriff's office and make sure the money is still there."

"The money?"

"Sheriff Darcy was going to count it and put it in his safe. Please, go, make sure it's there."

She begged him with her eyes and the indecision she saw in him would have to be enough. She ran past him and slipped out the back of the theater.

Gracie ran as hard and as fast as she could down Center Avenue, avoiding Main Street. This side of town was empty and dark. Block after block she ran. Most of the houses were dark as well. Halfway there, at Scott's Bluff Road, her lungs were bursting but she pushed on, only stopping when the church came into view.

Then she paused, resting her hands on her knees, taking several deep breaths to regain some strength. Gulping for air, she charged ahead. Her boots rubbing blisters, she raced around to the back of the church and skidded to a stop.

Gracie's heart sank. She found Stacy stuffing a cash box

into a saddle bag. Her sister froze at the sound of company but didn't say anything.

"That's the money, isn't it?"

Stacy's shoulders dropped as she appeared to relax. "It's you. How did you find me?"

"You think I forgot. We always hid our horses behind the church."

"I didn't think you'd remember that part." Stacy chuckled and lowered her head. "So, what gave me away?"

"You quoted Macbeth."

Stacy swore. "I surely did, didn't I?"

"And I thought I'd see you riding off across the plains. What delayed you?"

"The sheriff's safe." She snorted in disgust. "Tumblers were rusty. I thought I'd never get it open."

"But you did." Gracie walked up to her sister, glanced at her hand halfway in the saddle bag. "I can't let you leave with it."

"There's something else you can't do, little sister."

"What's that?"

"Stop me." Stacy whipped a .38 revolver free from the saddle bag and stepped back. In one smooth movement, she had it cocked and pointed it at Gracie's head. "All the fighting we did, I never thought we'd come to this."

"Put it down, Stacy." Gracie knew her sister was capable of pulling the trigger. The knowledge should have frightened her, but all she could think of was Betsy. A selfish, self-centered, egotistical actress wasn't going to stop the girl from getting to a doctor.

"I have to get out of Last Chance. If you try to stop me, I will kill you."

"I know. But I have to try."

The sound of footsteps and crunching gravel drew Gracie's attention, but Stacy's gaze did not waver. Gracie gasped and threw up a hand. "Stop, Matt. Get away from here."

The boy's eyes bugged. "I saw you run out the back. I knew—I knew something was wrong."

Stacy growled and spat another curse. "You understand, Gracie, I don't have any choice now."

Stacy swung the gun away from Gracie, who immediately lunged for it. The Colt belched thunder and fire. Wood exploded from the side of the church, barely above Matt's head.

"Run, Matt," Gracie screamed as she and Stacy wrestled for the gun. "Run!" The boy bolted like wolves were on his heels.

Tightening her grip on the gun, Gracie slipped her leg behind Stacy and buckled her knee. Unfortunately, Stacy kept hold of the .38 and took Gracie down with her. The gun fired again, the bullet zinging past the horse, who squealed in fear and tugged violently at the hitching rail.

"Give me the gun, Stacy."

"No, sister…"

The barrel was somewhere between them. It fired again and Gracie felt the streak of heat. *Oh, Jesus, please don't let either one of us die here tonight—*

Another gun fired, not Stacy's and both women stilled. "That's enough!" Noble's voice. Gracie could have cried with relief, but she clung tighter to Stacy's gun. "Let it go, ladies," he ordered.

Stacy and Gracie locked gazes. Both women sneered, scowled, but, finally Stacy sagged with defeat and released the gun. She rolled away from her sister. Tangled in her costume, Gracie started clawing her way to her feet when Noble grabbed her arm, helping her up. The sheriff did the same for Stacy.

"All right, you're both under arrest," Sheriff Darcy said, disappointment obvious in his tone.

"No," Matt yelled, lunging forward. "It's her." He pointed at Stacy. "She had the gun on Miss Gracie when I came around the corner and then she took a shot at me. It's not Miss Gra—"

"Matt," Gracie said gently. "Let the sheriff alone." She looked up at Noble. "I'm wanted for murder."

25

Gracie leaned her head back on the brick wall and closed her eyes. In the cell across from her, Stacy's glare was enough to heat the building. Not to mention, she hadn't stopped her vicious tirade from the moment the sheriff had dragged them in here and locked them up.

"I can't believe you're doing this to me, Gracie. I'm your sister."

"Not only did you try to kill me, you tried to kill Matt. That I won't forget."

"I'll say you were in on it. I'll tell them all."

"Then you should have had two horses at the church, not

one." Gracie sat up, curious about one thing. "How long? How long did you plan on stealing the money?"

Stacy sniffed in disgust. "From the moment you told me about the show. Though, honestly, I thought you'd help me." She seemed quite put-out by Gracie's lack of familial loyalty.

But those bonds were all but severed. Once again, Gracie closed her eyes and leaned back on the wall. Regardless, everything would come out in court. Stacy would go to jail for stealing. Gracie would go to jail for being an accomplice to murder. They would be old and gray when they got out.

At least Gracie'd had a good, decent life for a little bit. A hint of what love from a good man could be like. And a son who would, she was sure, make his parents proud. She would miss Noble and Matt so much, the thought could make her sob if she gave it free rein. But not here, not in front of Stacy.

She didn't hate her sister, but she remembered all the reasons why, when Melvin had proposed, leaving had seemed like a good idea. "At least we didn't die," she whispered. "And Betsy has her money. Thank you—" God. This desire to pray was probably just coming from the circumstances, but gratitude literally warred in her heart. "Thank you, Jesus."

"What are you doing over there?" Stacy sniped. "Praying? You *are* lost."

No, for the first time in her life, Gracie felt found. It made no sense. She couldn't explain it, but she had done the right thing, and she had peace. Once she made it to the women's prison, she would ask for a Bible and get to know Jesus better.

Metal clinked at the cell door and she looked up. Noble was unlocking the door. Gracie jumped to her feet. Stacy rushed to the front of her cell.

He swung open the door and grinned wide, mischief in his eyes…and something else that made her heart skip a beat. He offered her his big, calloused hand. "You're free, Gracie."

"What?"

"The man in Abilene was killed by his pard. The wanted poster was out of date, according to the marshal there." He cut his eyes at Stacy then back to Gracie. "And Matt told us what he saw. You tried to save his life."

"That's a lie," Stacy bellowed, clutching the cell bars with a white-knuckled grip. "She helped me steal the money. In fact, it was all her idea."

Noble dropped his hand, lowered his head for a moment, then walked over to Stacy's cell. He stared at her, long enough that she actually squirmed under his cold gaze. "You, Miss Medlin, are a miserable individual. I can't imagine stealing from a sick child, much less taking a shot at one." He leaned in and lowered his voice. "Good thing you missed." He let the statement hang in the air, until he turned back to Gracie and once again extended his hand. "Let's go home."

This time she didn't hesitate. She clutched his fingers and he pulled her in for a kiss. A long, desperate embrace full of freedom and promise. He knew everything and he still wanted her.

"Oh, dear God," Stacy spat and stomped away from the bars. Gracie didn't care. She had a new life in her arms and she clung tightly to him. And then she recalled her prayer.

God, if You're really there, if You really know me, please show me a way out of this…

Noble broke the kiss and stepped back. "Let's save this for home." He motioned to the cell door. "Lead the way."

Gracie ambled along the row of corn, hands in her pockets, shaking her head in amazement as she looked around the huge field. It was lush and green and the color had transformed the entire parcel near the creek into a vibrant, magical landscape. She marveled at the corn's height. Easily up to her elbows. She stopped to check a stalk, looking for a little ear. Nothing yet.

Noble slipped up behind her and locked his arms around her waist. She smiled and leaned back on him, almost overwhelmed with contentment. Some people would think that she had small dreams, but taking care of the man she loved, helping raise their son—and maybe more children—and running the theater in Last Chance, Nebraska suited her right down to her lace up boots.

She sighed and felt like purring, she was so happy. "I was only away, what, two days? Look how tall the corn is."

"Two days?" he repeated. "Oh, when you were performing in a play and going to jail?"

She reached back and smacked him playfully on the shoulder.

He held her a little tighter and whispered in her ear, "I'm sorry about your sister."

Gracie shrugged. "She never goes to jail for long. She'll put on an act for the judge and the good folks of Last Chance will show her mercy. She'll leave town and maybe I'll see her again one day. Maybe I won't. But I don't think I want to."

"I know I have no fondness for her."

"I ran away from home because of her. She filled my head with all these stories of how glamorous and exciting an acting troupe would be. She just needed someone in her group she could trust…and manipulate."

"That Gracie isn't around anymore."

She nodded but didn't reply. Her gaze drifted over to the edge of the horizon. The sun had set, but left behind a magnificent blaze of colors painted on the clouds. Nebraska had a beauty all its own.

"Millie stopped by today," she said. "Betsy and her mother are leaving tomorrow and they're quite hopeful about this new treatment. Betsy is going to be all right."

"Yes, she is," he said firmly. "I feel it in my bones."

"Well, that settles it then."

They chuckled, but the sound drifted off into the evening

air. She snuggled against him, astounded at the way she felt. So free, so light. No lies between them. Her heart was…clean. She had told Noble of her prayer. He'd told her of his prayers for her…then he'd asked her outright if she wanted to give her heart to Jesus. And just like that night at the tent revival in Dodge City, something came to life in her soul. On that night, she'd longed to walk the aisle, bow her knee to the Lord, make Him her king.

Noble had given her a second chance. She'd told him yes and then wept with inexplicable relief. He'd held her as she cried, the tears and Jesus washing away her past.

"Gracie, there's something I'd like to ask you."

She reflected how that question a few months ago would have frightened her. Now, she had nothing to hide from Noble. She spun around in his arms and gazed up at him. "Uhm?"

He drummed his fingers on her waist, cleared his throat, nodded. Gracie tilted her head, curious what was on his mind.

Suddenly, he dropped to one knee and clutched her hand. For a moment, she couldn't think. Her world was full of her handsome husband…his square jaw she wanted to kiss; hypnotic, dark eyes she hoped to see herself reflected in forever. She ran her hand through his wavy, caramel-colored hair…and froze. He was kneeling. *Kneeling.*

Her heart trip-hammered in her chest.

Noble drifted his thumb back and forth over her hand. "When we got married, we used the judge. That never felt right to me, Gracie. Will you do me the honor of marrying me…in a church? With a pastor?"

Her chin quivered and tears stung her eyes. "Yes." Would she ever get tired of crying from happiness? "Yes."

He rose, started to kiss her, but pulled back, a perplexed dip in his brow. "What is this?" With a fluid, easy movement, he plucked a gold ring from her ear…

She quit breathing. A ring. He had a ring for her. She blinked madly at her tears and reached for it. "Look at you, learning a new trick."

He moved the ring out of her reach. "No trick." His gaze steady, his voice husky with emotion, he said softly, "The real deal. You're my world now, Gracie. You and Matt. And I couldn't be happier."

With gentle, deliberate movements, he took her hand and slipped the ring on her finger. Gracie twisted the little, gold band around and around, marveling at its meaning. "Melvin never gave me a ring. He was afraid I'd forget to take it off. Somehow expose us as the frauds we were." She looked up at him. "I won't ever take this one off. Ever."

Noble cupped her chin and kissed her. "Glad we finally figured things out."

Gracie laughed, and hugged him, and then, arm in arm, they strolled back toward home.

DEAR READER, if you enjoyed getting to know the McCains, I would be so grateful for a review. It doesn't have to be long or wordy. Just share something that might bless other readers as they're considering this story. Thank you so much!

And be sure to check out book 12 in the Blizzard Brides series, *A Groom for Callie*!

ABOUT THE AUTHOR

"Heather Blanton is blessed with a natural storytelling ability, an 'old soul' wisdom, and wide expansive heart. Her characters are vividly drawn, and in the western settings where life can be hard, over quickly, and seemingly without meaning, she reveals Larger Hands holding everyone and everything together."

MARK RICHARD, *EXECUTIVE PRODUCER, AMC'S HELL ON WHEELS, and PEN/ERNEST HEMINGWAY AWARD WINNER*

A former journalist, Heather is an avid researcher and skillfully weaves truth in among fictional story lines. She loves exploring the American West, especially ghost towns and museums. She has walked parts of the Oregon Trail, ridden horses through the Rockies, climbed to the top of Independence Rock, and even held an outlaw's note in her hand.

She writes Westerns because she grew up on a steady diet of Bonanza, Gunsmoke, and John Wayne movies. Her most fond childhood memory is of sitting next to her father, munching on popcorn, and watching Lucas McCain unload that Winchester!

I *love* to hear from readers. You can **find me** several different ways.

Please consider signing up for my sassy, funny, sometimes politically incorrect newsletter at
authorheatherblanton.com
to get the latest news on new releases, events, parties, and other interesting bits of history! You'll receive a FREE story for subscribing!
I love **chatting** with book clubs, homeschool, and church groups. You can always **email me** directly
at *heatherblanton@ladiesindefiance.com* to set up a time! Thanks for reading! Blessings!

"I believe Christian fiction should be messy and gritty, because the human condition is ... and God loves us anyway."
-- Heather Blanton

ALSO BY HEATHER BLANTON

LOVE, LIES, & TYPEWRITERS

A cowboy with a Purple Heart. A reporter with a broken heart. Which one is her Mr. Right?

HELL-BENT ON BLESSINGS

"Though she be but little, she is fierce." Shakespeare

LOCKET FULL OF LOVE

Was her husband a traitor or a spy? A good man or a villain? The answer lies with the locket…

~Romance in the Rockies Series~the Box Set or…

A LADY IN DEFIANCE—Book 1

His town. Her god. Let the battle begin.

HEARTS IN DEFIANCE—Book 2

Men make mistakes. God will forgive them. Will their women?

A PROMISE IN DEFIANCE—Book 3

Choices have consequences. Even for the redeemed.

A DESTINY IN DEFIANCE—BOOK 4

Romances and rivalries are simmering in Defiance…

HOPE IN DEFIANCE

Two Choices. Neither one is wrong. But only one is her destiny.

~Brides of Evergreen Series~the Box Set or…

HANG YOUR HEART ON CHRISTMAS— Book 1

He wants justice—some say revenge. She wants peace. A deep betrayal may deny them everything.

ASK ME TO MARRY YOU— Book 2

Part I — Mail-Order Bride

Here comes the bride…and he's not happy

Part II — A Proposal so Magical

Sometimes, it takes a truly strong man to surrender

to love…

MAIL-ORDER DECEPTION—Book 3

Secret identities lead to stolen hearts.

Can love survive the truth?

TO LOVE AND TO HONOR—Book 4

Faith. Honor. Love. Which one will he sacrifice?

~Timeless Love/Time Travel~

IN TIME FOR CHRISTMAS – A NOVELLA

Charlene needs a miracle. God has one waiting …

a hundred years in the past.

FOR THE LOVE OF LIBERTY

She couldn't possibly be in love with a ghost, a mere shadow from the past.

But what if she is?

GRACE BE A LADY

Act like a man. Think like a lady.

~Sweethearts of Jubilee Springs Series~

A GOOD MAN COMES AROUND—Book 8

She has a list of qualifications for her groom.

He doesn't measure up.

A DISTANT HEART (Burning Dress Ranch Book 1)

She has a list of qualifications for her groom.

He doesn't measure up.

CAROLINA HOMECOMING (Thanksgiving Books & Blessings, Collection Three, 1)

Even in the shadows of the Blue Ridge, war will find them.

www.ingramcontent.com/pod-product-compliance
Lightning Source LLC
Chambersburg PA
CBHW021530150726

47990CB00006B/2174